PARADE OF HEARTS

"Now look what you've done!" Sara said, trying to smooth out the page. "My drawing is ruined!"

"Look, I'm really sorry," the boy said. "Is there any way to fix it?"

Sara looked up angrily. "I'll have to start all over and . . ." Her voice trailed off as she gazed into the most beautiful brown eyes she had ever seen.

"Are you all right?" the boy asked, reaching out to help her up.

Sara nervously scooped up her sketch pad and pencils and put her hand in his. As his fingers closed around hers, she felt even more embarrassed. "I'm fine," she stammered. "I was just a little shaken."

Sara pulled her hand away from his and clutched her pad to her chest. *He must be at least six-foot-two*, she thought, noticing his height. She looked into his eyes again. *How can any boy have such long eyelashes?*

Sara turned quickly and walked down the hill. She couldn't stay there another minute. Sara could feel him watching her as she hurried away. . . .

Here is a selection of
Bantam Sweet Dreams Romances
Ask your bookseller for the books you have missed

Parade of Hearts

Jahnna Beecham

BANTAM BOOKS
TORONTO · NEW YORK · LONDON · SYDNEY · AUCKLAND

RL 6, IL age 11 and up

PARADE OF HEARTS
A Bantam Book / February 1988

ISBN 0-553-26527-X

Bantam Books are published by Bantam Books, Inc. Its trademark, consisting of the words "Bantam Books" and the portrayal of a rooster, is Registered in U.S. Patent and Trademark Office and in other countries. Marca Registrada, Bantam Books, Inc., 666 Fifth Avenue, New York, New York 10103.

Reproduced, printed and bound in Great Britain by Hazell Watson & Viney Limited, Member of the BPCC Group, Aylesbury, Bucks

For Mom and Dad, with much love

Chapter One

Sara Arandel stepped on the black rubber mat, and the automatic doors swung open with a *whoosh!* As she walked outside, a blast of moist, hot air hit her like a warm washcloth. She dropped her suitcases onto the pavement and sighed wearily. Her arms ached from lugging her belongings around the airport, and the afternoon sun blazed down on her. She held up her hand to shield her eyes from the vicious glare of the sun as she looked out at the scene before her.

"Oklahoma," Sara muttered grimly. "The end of the world."

It looked awful! The airport was nothing but a bunch of drab boxlike buildings, all glass and harsh angles. Beyond it lay the runway, blistered with patches of sunburned weeds and grass along its edges. There were no trees or greenery anywhere. Sara almost expected to see tumbleweed roll by.

She fought the sudden urge to run back inside to take the first flight back to Vienna. *What am I doing here?* she asked herself dismally.

Sara checked her watch for the umpteenth time and desperately looked around for her aunt Dorsie. But there was no sign of her aunt anywhere. The few people who had gotten off the plane with her had already picked up their luggage and hurried off with their friends and families. Now the huge airport seemed deserted.

Where is she? Sara wondered impatiently. It had been over forty minutes since her plane had gotten in.

The trip from Austria had taken eighteen hours with changes and layovers, and Sara was exhausted. She caught a glimpse of herself in the glass windows of the terminal and winced. She looked as if she hadn't changed her clothes in three days.

Her white linen skirt and turquoise blouse were completely rumpled, and there was a tiny smudge of mascara under her right eye. But despite her wrinkled clothes, people would still say she was quite pretty—even striking.

She was fairly tall, and her thick brown hair, which fell halfway down her back, accentuated her height. But her deep blue eyes were the feature that people usually noticed first. They were almost royal blue and fringed with long, dark lashes.

Sara, however, was completely unaware of her beauty right then. She hadn't even noticed the two skycaps bump into each other as they watched her walk out of the terminal.

Sara reached into her canvas shoulder bag and pulled out the photograph her mother had given her before she left. It had been taken eight years before, the last time her family had visited Oklahoma. Sara couldn't help smiling as she looked at it.

Her mother and her aunt Dorsie were standing beside the porch swing, in front of Sara's grandmother's house. Her aunt, Doris Keating, was making a crazy face at the camera, and Sara's mother had her arm draped around her sister. She was laughing. It was hard for Sara to believe that they were sisters. They looked so different. Sara's mother was tall and thin, while her aunt was at least three inches shorter and definitely on the plump side. The only features they shared were their wide and friendly smiles.

A wave of homesickness swept over Sara as

she stared down at the picture. Her parents were halfway around the world in Vienna, and there she was, stranded in Oklahoma.

"A year at your grandmother's in the States will do you good," her mother had assured her. "You'll get to know the place where you were born. Besides," she had added, "your cousin Janie is just about your age. You two will have lots of fun together."

Sara knew how hard the decision to send her to live with her grandmother had been for her parents. They had agonized over it for weeks. As scientists for the United Nations, their jobs often took them away from their home in Vienna, but usually for just a week or two. Their new project, however, called for them to coordinate a huge soil-conservation program in western Africa. They'd be traveling for months at a time, hopping from one country to another.

"You've got to admit," her father had pointed out, "that gallivanting all over the Sahara Desert is not the best way to spend your senior year."

Sara knew they were right, although she couldn't help feeling a little abandoned. She hadn't lived in America since she was very young. And to say that life in Vienna was different from life in Oklahoma was the understatement of the century!

Sarah slipped the photo back into her bag, and with a huge sigh, she sat down on her suitcases. The heat was unbearable. Even her feet were hot and sweaty. She listlessly tried to smooth out the wrinkles in her skirt.

Beep! Beep! Startled by the sound, Sara looked up. A beat-up blue station wagon had swerved up the ramp and was heading toward her. The driver was honking wildly, and two other people were leaning out the windows, waving. Finally the car squealed to a halt in front of Sara, one wheel over the curb.

Sara stood up and stumbled backward over her suitcases, trying to get out of the way. The movement sent her purse flying out of her hand to the ground. As she bent over to pick it up, she heard someone shout, "Sara!"

Janie ran up to her first, hugging her and bouncing her up and down. Two more doors slammed, and suddenly Sara was engulfed by her aunt Dorsie and her grandmother as well.

Her aunt was going on about being late and how sorry she was. "And I can never seem to find my car keys. They just disappear!" she said, sounding baffled.

"Well, don't pester the girl with a lot of noise, Dorsie," Sara's grandmother said as

5

she hugged Sara warmly. "The important thing is that you're here and we're here and—oh, I can't believe how tall and pretty you've gotten."

Her grandmother looked just as Sara remembered her. She had white hair, sparkling blue eyes, and a laugh that sounded just like Sara's mother's. The one thing she hadn't remembered was her grandmother's Oklahoma twang. Her mother talked like that sometimes, but only when she was kidding around.

Janie broke into Sara's thoughts in an excited voice. "I can't believe you're finally here! I've got a million things to tell you!"

Janie had certainly changed since Sara had last seen her. Eight years before she had been a clumsy, energetic kid who was always getting into scrapes. She was still just as bubbly, but now more feminine and graceful. Her short brown hair really set off her brilliant green eyes, and she looked tan and muscular in her yellow shorts and flowered top.

Sara started to pick up her suitcases, but her aunt and Janie insisted on carrying them for her. Quickly they hustled her into the front seat of the car and drove away from the airport.

"Now we want to hear all about Vienna," her aunt said as she narrowly missed scraping the lane divider at the freeway entrance. "How are your parents?"

Before Sara could say a word, Janie leaned forward over the seat and announced, "Wait till the guys in Fort Reno see Sara. They're going to flip!"

Gran laughed and agreed. "She's just like her mother, a real heartbreaker!"

That comment set Dorsie off on a long reminiscence of the good old days when she and Sara's mother had started dating. Soon the three of them were chattering away gaily, paying little attention to whether Sara was listening or not. It gave Sara a chance to sit back a moment and try to absorb everything.

The sun was right in her eyes, so they had to be heading west. All of the buildings they passed seemed so spread out and empty—not at all like the crowded, winding streets of Vienna. They passed a sign off to the side which said, "Fort Reno—21, Amarillo—230, Albuquerque—515." Sara shook her head in disbelief. If you traveled five hundred miles in Europe, you could go through two or three countries, each with a totally different language and culture.

Try to keep an open mind, Sara silently reminded herself. But it was hard. She already missed Vienna dreadfully. It was home to her, and all her friends were there. She thought wistfully of the fun she had had wandering through the winding alleys in the old city, or ice-skating in the winter on the Danube Canal, or picnicking with her friends in the Vienna Woods. It was all just a memory now.

"That's Fort Reno High!" Janie yelled, and Sara suddenly snapped back to the present. Outside the window a clump of rectangular modern buildings, with a football field and track at one side, passed by. Sara felt a sudden flutter of nervousness as she realized that that was where she'd be spending her senior year.

They drove straight through the center of the town. As they went Janie and her grandmother acted like tour guides, calling out the names of all the stores they passed.

"On your left, is Burge's Drugstore," her grandmother said. "A real Fort Reno landmark."

Janie pointed to another store. "There's Proctor Appliance and Electric."

They both called out, "The Fort Reno Cinema!"

As Janie's mother turned right onto Walnut Street, all three chorused, "Our street!"

Sara edged forward expectantly, searching for her grandmother's house. As the car slowed to turn into the driveway, Sara looked up at the house. It was exactly as she had remembered it—a bright white frame house with green shutters and a big covered porch that wrapped around the front. Even the porch swing was still there.

The car lurched to a stop, and they all clambered out. Sara's aunt Dorsie opened the back of the station wagon, then suddenly cried out, "Oh, no! I forgot to defrost the chicken!"

She raced by them to unlock the door, calling over her shoulder, "Let's hope there's something else in the fridge."

"Doris Keating," her mother grumbled reprovingly as she trailed along after her, "sometimes I don't know what we're going to do about you!" As she passed Sara, she squeezed her arm and said, "I'll just check your room, to make sure Janie cleaned it up."

Sara picked up the suitcase Janie had dropped on the ground, feeling as though she had just been through a hurricane.

The sudden quiet seemed unnatural after all the commotion. Sara looped her purse over her shoulder, picked up two suitcases, and kicked the car door shut with her foot. As she reached the front steps, she noticed an old golden-colored dog lying on the grass in the neighbor's yard. He had witnessed the entire scene and was looking up expectantly, apparently hoping for more action.

"Here, boy!" Sara called. "Good dog."

He thumped his tail twice, then stretched out and rolled over to go to sleep.

She turned forlornly and mounted the steps of her new home. *How will I ever survive this year?* she wondered.

Right after dinner the girls had changed into their nightgowns, and Janie was helping Sara unpack. Sara tossed one of her suitcases on the bed and opened it, handing a pile of shirts to Janie.

The basement had been converted into a bedroom two years before, when Janie and her mother had come to live there. The cinderblock walls were painted a pale yellow, and bright flowered curtains hung over the tiny, high windows, making the room look more cheery. The bedspreads had the same pattern of red poppies and yellow daisies as the curtains. Janie had covered the walls with posters of her favorite rock groups.

Janie jokingly called the room the "Cave" because it was so dark. But she also quickly pointed out the advantages. "We have our own entrance," she said, motioning toward a door that led into the backyard. "It's practically like having our own apartment!"

Sara briefly wondered what sharing the basement room with her cousin would be like. Each was an only child and used to having her own room.

Janie walked across the room to her closet. "I've got cheerleading practice three mornings a week," she explained as she pushed her clothes to the side, making room for Sara's.

Sara neatly folded some shorts she had brought and tucked them into her half of the dresser. "You have to practice in the summer?"

Janie stopped what she was doing and stared at Sara. "Well, of course we do! We've got to be ready for the first game, just like the guys!" She went back to her bed and picked up a framed picture that she had on her bedside table. "We've been at it since the second week in June. In fact," she said, handing the picture to Sara, "we took first place at cheerleading camp."

Sara held the picture up to the light. It showed Janie and five other girls, all in blue-and-gold uniforms, posing with their trophy. Janie pointed out who each of the girls was.

"That's Caitlin, she's our captain." Sara looked at the pretty blonde holding the trophy. "And that's Michele. She and I are the only juniors on the squad. And then there's Louisa, Martha and Lizzie." Janie then sprang up in the air in a split, imitating her pose in the picture.

Sara laughed. "You look great!" She put the picture back on the table and added, "I'm sorry, I don't know much about cheerleaders. We didn't have them at my old school."

Janie dropped her arms and nearly fell over. "You're kidding!"

Sara shook her head. "No, I'm not. The school focused on the arts." She sat down on the twin bed across from Janie's. "We didn't even have team sports."

That did it as far as Janie was concerned. She collapsed on the floor and lay there staring at the ceiling. "I can't imagine school without football or cheerleading."

Sara grinned down at her. "Well, I can't imagine school with it. Besides, we never had time for sports. Most of the kids I knew took classes during the day and then studied or took more specialized classes at night."

Janie sat up, leaning back on her elbows. "It sounds awful."

Sara reached into her open suitcase and pulled out her sketch pad. "I loved it. I had this wonderful teacher that I took private drawing lessons from three times a week." She carefully unwrapped her wooden case where she kept her pencils and charcoals. "I wish I'd been able to go more often, but I had to allow some time for homework."

Janie watched Sara neatly arrange her art supplies on the dresser. "But what about guys? Or don't you date, either?"

Sara turned and stared at Janie. "Of course I date!"

"Where do you go?" Janie asked. "I mean, what do you do for fun?"

"We go to movies and plays and dances, just like in America." She walked back to the bed and closed her suitcase.

"Yeah, but isn't it all in German?"

Sara sat on the bed. "Not everything," she replied. "Some movies are in English, but a lot of times they're dubbed."

Janie rolled her eyes. "What about TV? They *do* have TV over there, don't they?"

Sara laughed. "Of course we have TV! In fact, there's one really popular American show that I like. Translated, the name is 'Denver Clan.' "

"I've never heard of it," Janie said, perplexed.

"Over here it's called 'Dynasty,' " Sara explained.

"You're kidding!" Janie yelled.

Sara nodded. "I can't wait to see it. I've never heard it in English."

Janie leaned back against the bed. "Wow! I can't imagine the show in German." She shrugged. "I guess I can't imagine speaking in anything but English." She looked up at Sara and asked, "Did you speak German in Vienna?"

"Yes," Sara said, smiling. "When you go shopping and stuff, you have to. But at my school, since the kids came from a lot of different countries, we all spoke to each other in English."

"So," Janie asked, changing the subject, "do you have a boyfriend?"

"Not really," Sara said as she stood up to finish unpacking. "But there is one guy . . ."

"Oh?" Janie leaned forward with interest. "What's his name?"

Sara blushed and ran her hand through her hair. "Well, I don't know him very well, but he's walked with me to class a couple of times."

Janie giggled and looked up into Sara's face. "Come on, what's his name?"

"Wulf," Sara said, pronouncing the *w* like a *v*.

"Wolf? His name is Wolf?" Janie cried. "Who would name their son Wolf?"

"It's a very common Austrian name," Sara said as she tossed the suitcase under the bed.

But Janie just giggled. Sara tried to explain that Wulf was as common a name as John or Mike would be in America. But every time she said the name, Janie would start laughing all over again. Janie's laugh was so infectious that Sara gave up and started giggling, too.

She finally caught her breath. "Boy, things really are different here."

Janie, still on the floor, leaned her back against her bed and nodded.

A moment later Sara asked in a quiet voice, "Do you think I'll ever fit in?"

"Of course." Janie reached up and squeezed Sara's hand and confided, "You know, after my parents' divorce, I begged my mom to let us stay in Albuquerque. But she had her heart set on coming back to her hometown. It was probably a little easier for me than for you because we'd spent so many vacations here already." She smiled reassuringly. "But I just know my friends are going to love you!" Sara could only manage a feeble smile.

"And," Janie added, springing to her feet,

"you're going to meet everybody who's anybody next Friday."

"What?" Sara felt another twinge of nervousness.

"I signed you up to work on the Sooner Days committee. It's the big event of the summer, and I know it'll be terrific."

"But—but—" Sara stammered.

Janie held up a hand to silence her cousin. "Don't panic. I'll be there, too. All the juniors and seniors from school will be working on it. We'll be planning the dance and parade. The dance is on Friday—four weeks from today. And the parade is the next day."

Sara had always been shy in big groups, even when she knew everyone. The idea of joining a committee where she didn't know anyone terrified her. "Listen, Janie, I'm not so sure I want to—"

"Come on, you'll have a great time. And besides," Janie said, putting both hands on her hips, "when you're trying to meet people, the best thing to do is just dive in!"

"But I don't even know what Sooner Days is!" Sara persisted.

Janie dropped her arms to her sides and said, "Well, I'll tell you what it is." Sara watched as Janie settled herself cross-legged on her bed. "In 1889 there was a land rush.

16

People lined up in covered wagons and on horses, and when someone in the government fired a gun they all charged into Oklahoma to stake out their land. But"—she leaned forward—"some people couldn't wait and sneaked in early to claim the best spots. They were called Sooners because they got here *sooner* than everyone else. That's why Oklahoma is called the Sooner State."

Sara, remembering the bleak countryside, joked halfheartedly, "What was their big hurry?"

Janie laughed and went off to the bathroom to brush her teeth. When she got back, she turned to Sara and said earnestly, "Look, I know that Fort Reno may not look like much on the surface." She slid into bed and added with an impish grin, "But sooner or later, Sara, you're going to love it here!"

Sara tucked her legs under the sheets and flicked off her bedside lamp. She nestled her head into her pillow, exhausted from all her traveling. As Sara drifted off to sleep, her mind whirled with visions of airplanes and covered wagons and cheerleaders all chasing her toward Fort Reno.

Chapter Two

Sara glanced at her watch and squinted up at the sun. It was three o'clock. *Only four more hours till the big meeting*, she thought. A nervous bolt of panic shot through her.

Sara put her sketch pad down on the grassy hillside next to her and stretched her arms out wide. Her thick braid bounced on her shoulders as she shook her head and looked out at the horizon. Fort Reno, Oklahoma. Had she been there for only seven days? It felt like a lifetime.

She had spent the week getting to know the town. On Tuesday her aunt and grandmother gave her the grand tour, which included the public library, the Presbyterian church, and the municipal golf course. They topped the day off with an ice-cream sundae at a place called The Scoop.

The Scoop was one of those old-fashioned ice-cream parlors that Sara had always read about. They sat at the counter on worn red leather stools that spun around. The soda fountain was huge and made of beautiful polished wood. An enormous beveled mirror covered the back wall.

Sara's aunt had insisted on ordering banana splits for all of them. She then proceeded to describe, in great detail, her new diet. Waving her spoon at their banana splits, she said, "Why, the fudge topping alone must be at least a thousand calories. Do you know how many sit-ups you'll have to do to burn that off?" She shook her head in awe at the idea and dipped back into her ice cream. "It makes me tired just thinking about it."

Gran slammed her spoon down on the counter. "Doris Keating, if you are so gung-ho about your new diet, what in the world are you doing eating a banana split?"

Her daughter paused with her spoon halfway to her mouth. "What did you expect me to order at an ice-cream parlor—a scoop of cottage cheese on a rye cracker?" She dug into her banana, adding righteously, "I'm only doing this for Sara."

Sara chuckled to herself. Her grandmother and aunt cracked her up. They were forever getting into harmless tiffs, each goading the other. In fact, the entire household seemed to operate at a fever pitch—with phones ringing, doors crashing, and the TV blasting at all hours. And her aunt and grandmother were both involved in a hundred different clubs. They were always rushing off to some meeting or other. Just as the house would quiet down, Janie would charge through on her way to cheerleading practice, leaving a trail of clothes behind her. Sara smiled. *Never a dull moment!* she thought. Still, sometimes the frenzied energy level was too much for her.

Luckily, Sara had discovered a little park by the Rock Island train trestle. She had been going there to sketch and think nearly every day since she found it.

A grassy hill sloped up to the track, and from the top Sara had a view of the entire park. That day the fenced playground off to the right was filled with toddlers. Their mothers sat clustered in groups, chatting lazily, yet still managing to keep one eye trained on their children. There were two tennis courts off to the left, and Sara watched a couple of older women in bulging sweat suits lob balls at each other. They spent most of their time chasing the balls, instead of hitting them.

Just below Sara, in a wide grassy area, some boys were tossing a Frisbee. They looked like they were about her age, so she leaned forward and watched their game. All of them seemed to be quite nice looking, but one particular boy caught her eye. He was tall and tan, with sun-streaked hair, and there was an ease and confidence in his movements that set him apart from the others. His crisp white tennis shorts and striped polo shirt made him look like the perfect all-American boy.

"Hey, Brad!" One of the guys yelled to him. "Go long!"

"Brad," Sara whispered. It was a good name, she thought. She watched him leap into the air, catching the Frisbee with one hand. He threw his head back and laughed as he wound up to return the toss. His smile was heart stopping, and Sara found herself smoothing her hair and tucking her shirt back into her khaki cotton shorts, hoping he'd look her way.

A slight summer breeze ruffled the leaves in the tree behind her, and Sara shook her head. *What am I doing?* she wondered. *He's probably already got a girlfriend.*

She picked up her pad and turned her attention back to her drawing. It was a charcoal sketch of the Belvedere Palace in Vienna. The palace had been built for Prince Eugene of Savoy. He had saved the Viennese from the invading Turkish army, and a grateful Austrian emperor gave him the Belvedere. Sara thought it was the most beautiful place she had ever seen.

She closed her eyes and tried to remember every detail of the palace—the big beautiful mansion, with its sea-foam green roof, the ornate carved fountains, which created rainbows in their spray, the elegant manicured gardens that stretched down toward the city. From the palace steps, you could see the whole skyline of Vienna, with the great dome of St. Stephen's Cathedral surrounded by the slim spires of scores of smaller churches that dotted the city.

There were also two huge statues guarding the palace steps. Sara squeezed her eyes tight, trying to remember what they looked like. Then she recalled them—fantastic mythological creatures, almost like harpies. They had wings and armor, but were half woman and half lion. A smile touched her lips. How could she ever have forgotten them?

The sound of footsteps nearby shook Sara

from her thoughts. She opened her eyes just in time to see a figure stumbling backward up the hill toward her. At the same moment the bright yellow Frisbee skidded across her drawing.

The sudden noise frightened her. She tossed the pad in the air and leaped to her feet. "Why don't you watch what you're doing?"

She heard a male voice apologizing, but she was too busy retrieving her sketch pad to look up at him. He had tripped on it, and the page was crumpled.

Sara fell to her knees. "Now look what you've done!" she said, trying to smooth out the page. "My drawing is ruined!"

"Look, I'm really sorry," the boy said. "Is there any way to fix it?"

Sara looked up angrily. "I'll just have to start all over and . . ." Her voice trailed off as she gazed into the most beautiful brown eyes she had ever seen.

The whole world seemed suddenly to stand still as she knelt there staring into his handsome face. She almost said "Brad," but quickly stopped herself.

Sara's face burned with embarrassment. She had just acted like a complete jerk!

"Are you all right?" he asked, reaching out to help her up.

24

She nervously scooped up her sketch pad and pencils and put her hand in his. As his fingers closed around hers, she felt even more embarrassed. "I'm fine," she stammered. "I was just a little shaken."

Sara pulled her hand away from his and clutched her pad to her chest. *He's much taller than I am,* she thought, noticing Brad's height. *He must be at least six-foot-two.* She looked into his eyes again. *How can any boy have such long eyelashes?*

"Um, don't worry about the drawing," she finally said, backing away. "I can always do another one."

As he bent over to pick up the Frisbee, Sara turned and quickly walked down the hill. She couldn't stay there another minute. Sara could feel him watching her as she hurried away, and she tried hard not to look as rattled as she felt. But it didn't really matter. Even if he saw her trip and fall, she knew she couldn't appear any dumber than she already did.

After the trauma of the afternoon, Sara wasn't too thrilled about meeting any more people. But Janie insisted. Reluctantly, Sara got ready for the evening.

She put on a pair of pleated tan pants and

a T-shirt with bright splotches of red, yellow, and blue that she had painted herself. She threw a red cotton shirt over her T-shirt and turned up the collar, then slipped into her red ballerina flats. She quickly ran a brush through her hair and took one last look in the mirror.

"You look *trés chic*," Janie said, studying her own reflection over Sara's shoulder.

"So do you," Sara said, stepping back to give Janie the mirror. "That looks brand-new," she commented. Janie was wearing pale yellow overalls and a white, cotton knit shirt.

"It is," Janie said, adjusting one of the straps on her shoulder. "I thought this would be a good chance to show it off."

Sara watched Janie move around the room, brushing her hair and squirting cologne behind her ears. She was dying to tell her cousin about the boy she had met in the park. Sara was certain that Janie must know him. But then, she was also pretty sure that he must have a girlfriend. He probably went out with a cheerleader—one of those girls in Janie's picture. She'd be small and bubbly, with a big smile—someone who rooted for him at football games, if he played football. No, Sara thought, he wasn't the football type. He looked more like a basketball player, very lean and muscular. He looked like the kind of guy that all the kids knew and admired—exactly the kind she had never met.

On the other hand, Sara told herself encouragingly, he could be a newcomer like me. Maybe he just happened to be strolling through the park and got involved in the Frisbee game. Maybe at that very moment, someone was dragging him to the same silly meeting. Maybe she'd even see him there, and they could sneak out together. Maybe they would discover they were perfect for each other, and then they could run away from Oklahoma and travel all over the world. Maybe—

"Earth to Sara," Janie said, waving her hand in front of Sara's face.

"What?" Sara asked as she looked up with a start.

"I've been talking to you for the past five minutes, and you haven't heard a word I've said—have you?"

"I'm sorry, I guess I was daydreaming," Sara apologized. *Daydreaming is an understatement!* she thought.

Sara shook her head and looked at Janie. "What were you saying?"

"Just that the Martians have landed and

we're under attack." She crossed her eyes at Sara. "You know, nothing important."

Sara laughed and took one last look in the mirror.

"Ready?" Janie asked.

Sara gave her cousin an anxious smile. "As ready as I'll ever be!"

When they reached Fort Reno High, Janie gave Sara a quick pep talk. "Now remember, just dive in! I was new two years ago, and look how far I've gotten!" She reached for the gym door and flung it open.

The noise was deafening. Kids were huddled together in groups, and it seemed as though everyone was talking at once. Their voices echoed loudly in the gym. Sara started to turn around to leave, but Janie grabbed her arm and dragged her into the crowd.

The first person Sara met was Caitlin O'Donnel, a petite blonde with perfectly styled, collar-length hair and a cute turned-up nose. Sara recognized her as the one with the trophy in Janie's photo.

"So you're Janie's cousin," Caitlin said in a soft voice. "She's told us all about you!" She turned and nudged Janie in the ribs. "You didn't say she was such a knockout. Competition!" Caitlin radiated confidence, and Sara felt like an awkward giraffe standing next to her.

"Hi, I'm Caroline Griffin," a tall, heavyset girl said as she came up to Sara.

Janie draped her arm over Caroline's shoulder and said, "She's our pep club president, and all-around chairperson of everything."

Caroline laughed boisterously. She was wearing a blue T-shirt that said "Here Comes the Cavalry" in gold letters, and her dark hair was tucked under a red baseball cap.

"I'm currently chairman of the dance committee," Caroline said with a friendly smile. "I'd love it if you'd join us. We could use a new face." Sara liked her instantly.

Before Sara could say anything, Janie spun her around and introduced her to four more girls. "Meet the cheerleading squad!" They were all cute and bouncy, just like Janie.

Janie grabbed Sara's arm and pulled her off to meet another group. Suddenly she froze and whispered, "There he is!"

"Who?" Sara asked, looking around her.

"Judd Parkin, over there by the door with Peter Silbert."

Sara saw the boys standing at the gym entrance. One was short and muscular, with thick black hair. The other wore wire-rim glasses and slumped comfortably against the wall.

"He is such a hunk!" Janie gushed.

Sara craned her neck to get a better look. "The dark-haired one?"

Janie nodded. "With the blue, blue eyes. I've had a crush on him for two years."

Sara watched him saunter through the crowd in his cowboy boots and jeans. He moved like a football player with his arms held slightly away from his body. She whispered back to Janie, "He's really handsome!"

Janie's eyes lit up. "I'll be right back," she said hurriedly and sailed off in his direction.

Sara stood there, trying to look as inconspicuous as possible. She kept shoving her hands in the pockets of her pants and then taking them out, as she inched her way toward the wall of the gym.

"You look lost," Caroline said, coming up and hooking her arm in Sara's. "Come on, I'll introduce you to our student council president."

Sara, relieved to see a familiar face, smiled shyly. "Thanks. I guess I feel a little overwhelmed. There are so many new names and faces to remember."

Caroline led her toward the stage at the far end of the gym. She smiled and waved to everyone they passed, calling out, "This is Janie's cousin, Sara. She's from Vienna."

Sara felt like a toy during show-and-tell. Her face was frozen in a permanent smile, and she kept bobbing her head up and down as they made their way across the gym.

"There he is!" Caroline announced. She quickened her pace, pulling Sara toward the boy who was leaning casually against the stage. He was wearing faded jeans and sneakers. His pale yellow T-shirt showed off his muscular, tanned arms, and his head was bent as he concentrated on some papers.

Sara couldn't see his face, but she knew who it was: Brad, the boy from the park! Her heart pounded in her chest, and she frantically searched for something to say to him to make up for her rudeness earlier. Without her realizing it, Sara's knees locked. Caroline's quick tug on her arm caused her to stumble forward.

Brad looked up just in time to see Sara, with her arms flailing, try to catch her balance. He quickly reached out to steady her, and for the second time that day, their eyes met.

"Brad," Caroline bubbled, "I want you to meet—"

"We've already met," Brad interrupted. He

put his papers down and added, with a twinkle in his eye, "Or I guess I should say, we've bumped into each other before." He reached out to shake Sara's hand. "Hi, I'm Brad Ayres."

Sara, still flustered, reached out and said, "I'm—uh—I'm Sara Arandel." She shook his hand, hoping he couldn't tell that she was a mass of Jell-O inside.

"Did you just move here?" he asked, his warm brown eyes studying her face.

She clutched her hands tightly in front of her and stammered, "Kind of. I'm staying with my grandmother for the school year. At least I think so. I'm not really sure how long I'll be here."

"Well, let's hope it's not for too long," another voice piped in. "We Fort Reno girls don't need the competition."

Sara turned to see Caitlin, who winked at her knowingly. Another surge of heat covered Sara's face. Caitlin had just watched her act like a total babbling idiot!

Just then, Brad hopped onto the stage and flicked the microphone on. He called the meeting to order and made the announcements about who would be heading what committee. The names were unfamiliar, so Sara didn't pay close attention. All she could do was stare at him. He was so handsome and self-assured in front of all those people.

Sara's ears did perk up when she heard him say, "I'll be heading the parade float committee, and I'm sure it's going to be a winner this year!" All the kids cheered, and Sara found herself shouting along with everyone else.

At the end of the meeting, Sara determinedly pushed her way toward the sign-up sheets. She found the yellow-lined page at the table with the sign that said "Float Committee."

Caitlin's name was first on the list. As Sara reached for the pen, she felt a stab of guilt. Caroline had asked her to be on the dance committee. Then she thought of Brad's liquid brown eyes and hastily signed her name under Caitlin's. Janie had said to just dive in, and that was just what she was going to do. She giggled to herself, thinking, *Once I'm in the pool, I hope I can swim.* She spotted Janie on the other side of the gym and practically skipped toward her.

Chapter Three

"Now listen," Sara's aunt Dorsie said, peering over the top of her reading glasses. "Gran has her literary club tonight, and I won't be home for dinner, either. You two are on your own, OK?"

Sara watched as she emptied the contents of her overstuffed purse onto the kitchen table. Bobby pins, gum wrappers, pennies, a pair of scissors, a spool of thread, and a billfold came pouring out. Then she pulled out a kitchen chair and sat down, still digging in her purse. "Unfortunately, I have everything in here but what I need!"

Sara rested her chin on her hand, smiling at her aunt. With her head bent over her purse, she looked a lot like Sara's mother. But they were so different. Her mother was incredibly organized, with everything always in its place. Their house in Vienna was always neat, and uncluttered. She glanced around her grandmother's kitchen. The pans and dishes stacked in the dish drainer were on the verge of collapsing into the sink. Messages, attached by little fruit magnets and Scotch Tape, covered the refrigerator, and none of the wooden kitchen chairs matched. But all the same, the room had a warm, cozy feel about it. It always smelled good, too—like fresh toast.

"Aha!" her aunt finally announced. She triumphantly held up a worn leather change purse that had "Mom" beaded on it. Janie must have given it to her years before.

"Here's twelve dollars," she said, handing Sara a wad of bills she had pulled from the change purse. She removed her glasses, letting them dangle from the chain around her neck. "You make Janie take you to a nice place for dinner."

Sara took the money and helped her aunt scoop her belongings back into her flowered tapestry bag.

Her aunt Dorsie glanced at the kitchen clock hanging at an angle over the doorway. "My ride will be here any minute." Sara followed her into the living room. "I'm going to give you the car keys, if I can find them, and I want you to promise to make sure Janie drives safely." She tossed her purse on the couch and started rummaging all over again. "She's only had her license for three months, and I worry about her."

Sara put one hand over her heart and said solemnly, "I promise."

"Maybe you should drive," her aunt muttered, slipping her glasses back onto her nose. "You're much more level-headed than Janie, and I'll bet you're a better driver, too." She lifted one of the couch cushions and groped under it.

"I'd like to," Sara said, "but in Austria, you can't get a license until you're eighteen."

"That makes good sense to me," her aunt said as she counted the change she had just found under the cushions.

Sara watched her aunt start shuffling through the magazines that were spread out on the table and decided to join in the search. She had only been living there a short while, but she was starting to know the routine.

"What you need," Sara said as she headed for her aunt's bedroom, "is one of those beepers that announces where the keys are!"

"That wouldn't help," her aunt called from the other room. "With my luck I'd lose the beeper!"

Sara laughed in response and searched the dresser top. She checked the bathroom sink and peeked into her grandmother's room. Then on a sudden impulse, she headed for the front door.

"Here they are!" Sara shouted as she pulled the keys out of the lock.

Her aunt, who was on her knees peering behind the couch, pulled herself up. "Did I do that again?" she asked, tugging at her red- and blue-striped blouse. "Why, a burglar could have just walked in, taken the TV, and then driven off with it in the car!"

A horn beeped out front, and she charged for the door. Sara scooped up the tapestry bag from the couch and raced down the porch steps after her. Her aunt took her purse, gave Sara a quick hug, and leaped into the car.

Sara stood in the middle of the street waving goodbye and shaking her head. "This sure is a crazy house!" she said with a sigh.

She took a few steps to the right and peered down the alley between the neighbors' houses. From there she had a clear view of the park by the Rock Island train trestle. Sara could see some guys tossing a football off in the distance, and she wondered if Brad might be one of them. She had gone there for the past three days hoping to catch a glimpse of him, but he hadn't appeared.

Sara hummed as she skipped up the porch steps. The next day at the float committee meeting, she would see him for sure.

Inside the house, Sara paused to look at herself in the hall mirror. As she twisted her long, dark hair into a knot high on her head, she wondered what Brad thought of her. Sara stood and earnestly studied her reflection, tilting her chin over her shoulder. She tried to visualize herself staring dreamily into Brad's eyes. She fluttered her lashes and drawled, "Oh, Brad!" in her most sultry voice.

Then, the image of Caitlin, with her pert nose and soft blond hair, flashed through Sara's mind. She let her hair fall straight around her face, scrunched up her nose, and stuck her tongue out at herself.

"Hey, where is everybody?" Janie called, slamming the back screen door.

Sara peeked sheepishly around the corner. "In here, Janie!"

When Sara broke the news that they had the car and twelve dollars to spend on dinner, Janie was thrilled.

"I know the absolute perfect place!" She raced down the stairs to their room and changed out of her sweat pants. Sara followed her. *Nobody in this house stays in one room long enough to finish a complete sentence,* she thought as she went down the steps.

She watched as Janie tossed clothes out of the dresser. "Should I change, too?" she asked. "How fancy is it?"

Janie stopped and looked at Sara, seriously studying her appearance. "I think what you've got on will be just fine."

Sara was wearing khaki shorts and a Hawaiian shirt. Janie threw on a pair of baggy white pants and an electric blue camp shirt.

They grabbed the car keys and pulled the front door shut. Finally Sara couldn't stand the suspense any longer. "Janie, where are we going?" she blurted out.

Janie tossed the keys in the air and said casually, "The Sonic Drive-In, of course!" She laughed and then jumped from the porch to the ground.

Sara put her hands on her hips and asked, "The Sonic Drive-In?"

Janie just ignored her. She yanked open the car door and scooted behind the wheel. "They have the best burgers in all of Oklahoma." The sound of the engine starting muffled the rest of her words, but Sara was pretty sure she had said, "It's absolutely *the* in hangout!"

As they drove down Walnut Street, Janie chattered away about cheerleading practice. Sara wished her cousin would look at the road when she talked, instead of at her.

At the stop sign, Janie announced, "Well, Sara, you're the hottest topic in town these days. All the girls on the squad think you're gorgeous." She signaled for a left and promptly turned right onto Main Street. "Even Caitlin is starting to get nervous."

Keeping her eyes glued to the road since Janie's weren't, Sara asked, "Why would she be nervous about me?"

"Caitlin noticed the way Brad looked at you on Friday, and she wasn't too happy about it."

Sara felt a mixture of excitement and jealousy. She took her eyes off the road and looked at Janie. "I didn't know they were a couple."

"They're not," Janie turned left at the light, one wheel of the car nudging the curb. "But Caitlin has made it clear that she's going after Brad." Janie looked meaningfully at Sara. "And what Caitlin wants, Caitlin usually gets."

Sara shrugged and tried to sound casual. "Well, she shouldn't worry about me. I don't even know Brad." She almost added, "I wish I did," but she didn't.

A few cars were already lined up under the pink- and purple-striped awning when they pulled in to the Sonic Drive-In. The building itself was painted lime green and was covered with bright pink polka dots. There were picnic tables on a center island, and music blasted out of speakers that hung under the awning.

Janie reached out her window, pushed the button on the rusted silver intercom, and ordered "Two Sonic Specials with everything on them." Then she turned to Sara. "Isn't this place the greatest?"

Sara was appalled at the color scheme, but she managed to say, "It certainly is out-of-this-world!"

"Oh, look, there's Caroline!" Janie cried, hitting the horn in one long beep. Caroline beeped back, which set the whole drive-in honking for a couple of minutes.

Sara covered her ears and watched Suzanna, one of the carhops, rush toward the car. Her uniform was as bright as everything else in the drive-in, and her name was neatly stitched in shocking pink over the pocket of the striped shirt.

She brushed her hand through her short

blond curls and leaned in Sara's side of the car. "Janie, have you heard the latest?"

"No, what?" Janie asked breathlessly as she turned to look at Suzanna.

Sara flattened herself against the seat to let them talk. Her head turned from one to the other as they chattered.

"Well," Suzanna said, lowering her voice, "a bunch of the guys have thought up something great to pull on Brisco High."

Janie nudged Sara. "They're our biggest rival," she said.

Suzanna nodded in agreement and quickly continued. "Anyway, Judd's heading it, and they have announced that absolutely no girls can go along."

Janie's eyes lit up at the mention of Judd's name. "When's it going to happen?"

"A week from Thursday night!" A bell sounded and Suzanna turned and yelled, "Coming!" toward the lime green building. She ducked her head back in the window, "Listen, I've got an order to deliver. Get Caroline to tell you about it."

Sara watched Suzanna gesture toward Caroline and then rush off. A few minutes later another girl who was wearing the same black pants and pink- and purple-striped shirt as Suzanna delivered their Sonic Specials.

Moments later Caroline walked over to Janie's side of the car. She waved hello to Sara. She leaned with one arm on the roof of the car, whispering to Janie. Sara couldn't quite make out what Caroline was saying.

She didn't want to seem as though she was eavesdropping, so she turned her attention to her hamburger. It was huge. No matter how carefully she held it, ketchup and mustard oozed out and dropped onto her lap whenever she took a bite. Out of the corner of her eye she watched Janie eating her burger, not spilling a drop.

Sara listened to Janie exclaim, "You're kidding!" and, "That's fantastic!" She was dying of curiosity and longed to be included. The problem was, she couldn't think of a thing to say. Sara had never heard of Brisco High, and she had only met Caroline once. In fact, the whole world of cheerleading and school spirit and even drive-ins was completely foreign to her.

In Vienna she rode the streetcars, or *Strassenbahn*, *everywhere. Sometimes after school, Sara and her friends would hop on the number two down to the* Opernring, *the grand boulevard in front of the opera house, to window-shop. Or they'd go to a konditorei,* a pastry shop, and order apple strudel. Maybe, on special occasions, they'd have a Sacher torte, the great Viennese chocolate cake. Then they would linger over their coffee or apple juice for hours, listening to classical music and trading gossip. Sara took a slow sip of her root beer and sighed. Her friends were so far away!

A glob of mustard splattered on her leg. She absentmindedly scooped it up and leaned against the armrest. The drive-in was really starting to get crowded. Kids were draped on cars, laughing and chatting. The picnic tables were packed with people all trying to be heard over the music that blared from the speakers. It was certainly the *in* spot, and Sara felt completely *out* of it.

A high-pitched giggle came from the car next to her, and Sara turned her head to look. A tall, sandy-haired boy was leaning against the front fender. His arms were wrapped around a perky brunette, who giggled every time he whispered in her ear.

He looked a little bit like Brad, Sara thought. But Brad was ten times better looking. She smiled wistfully, thinking of Brad's twinkling brown eyes. Sara pictured him leaning against his car whispering into her ear, and her arms tingled with goose bumps.

Suddenly Sara sprang up in her seat, bumping her head on the door frame. While she was daydreaming, she had let her cup of root beer slip in her hand. It spilled all over her lap. She grabbed a paper napkin and angrily dabbed at the drops of root beer.

What was I thinking about? I don't even know if Brad has a car! She tossed an ice cube out of the window. *We've spoken exactly twice, and I've sounded like an idiot both times.*

Sara was squirming in her seat, trying to sweep the ice cubes out from under her, when she realized she was being watched. She heard the perky brunette giggle again and looked up. Waving feebly at the grinning couple, she tried to manage a smile as she felt the red rise to the roots of her hair.

Chapter Four

"You're on your own!" Janie shouted as she dropped Sara off in the school parking lot the next evening. "Good luck!"

Sara waved back forlornly, watching the blue station wagon weave through the parking lot to head for Main Street. She fumbled for her brush in her purse. As she ran it briskly through her hair one last time, she muttered, "I'm on my own."

Sara took a deep breath and reached for the gym door. She boldly pulled it open and saw about twenty people seated in the chairs at the far end of the gym. The meeting had obviously just started. Sara quickly glanced at her watch. It was exactly seven o'clock. She scolded herself for not getting there earlier as she self-consciously tiptoed across the wooden floor.

There was an empty seat in the back, and Sara slid into it as quietly as she could. But as she did, one of her heels caught on the leg of the metal folding chair, making a loud *gong.* Some of the kids turned to look at her. She smiled shyly at them and then looked toward the front of the room.

"The theme for the parade," Brad was saying, "is Oklahoma: Yesterday and Today." He was seated on a chair in front, his ankle crossed on the knee of his other leg. He was balancing a clipboard on his leg. He folded up the sleeve of his shirt and continued. "Schools from around the country will be competing, and this will be a great opportunity for Fort Reno to show Brisco High who's number one."

Everybody applauded. Sara heard a lilting voice pipe up, "We've been working on some other ways, too!"

She leaned to one side and saw Caitlin and a small group of her friends all laugh knowingly. Caitlin was sitting directly in front of Brad, and she looked like she had just stepped out of a fashion magazine. Suzanna, the girl from the Sonic Drive-In, was sitting next to her.

"The first order of business is to come up with a winning idea," Brad said. "So let me introduce Fort Reno High's resident artist and all-around genius." He gestured to his left. "Ro-b-b-b Proctor!"

Once again everyone clapped. A few guys called out, "Way to go, 'Doctor' Proctor!"

Sara hadn't even noticed the thin, redheaded boy standing next to Brad. His wiry hair seemed to go every which way, and tons of freckles covered his long gaunt face. He looked kind of goofy. A sketch pad was tucked under his arm, and he shuffled his feet and smiled crookedly at the group.

Rob spoke with a thick southern accent. "Well, I've been thinking about this one idea," he said, scratching his head. "And I've made a few sketches. So I'll just show them to you, and y'all can tell me what you think."

Sara watched him unfold his pad and prop it up on a black music stand. The drawing was done in ink and watercolor and looked like a finished painting. Sara craned her neck to see it better. *He's terrific*, she thought.

"In the center of the flatbed, we'll put General Sheridan, on a white charger carrying the flags of the United States and Oklahoma." Rob stopped and looked at the group. "The horse would be made out of chicken wire."

49

A couple of kids moaned at the thought of stuffing thousands of paper napkins into the chicken wire framework.

"The general would be made out of plaster of Paris."

"It wouldn't be the first time he'd been plastered!" Peter Silbert cracked.

Rob made a face and stepped to the side of his sketch. "Behind him, Peter, would be cardboard cutouts of the cavalry."

Someone from the group yelled, "Charge!" and everyone joined in cheering. Brad held up his hands to quiet the group, and Rob continued.

"The cavalry would start out as the real ones in their uniforms. Each succeeding pair would be dressed in costume from a later period until the ones at the end would be us." He made a sweeping gesture to everyone, "The cavalry from Fort Reno High School!"

Brad enthusiastically joined in. "So the heroes from the past become our country's hope for the future!"

Rob nodded. "Exactly!"

"I get it!" Suzanna blurted out. "Students would be pictured as scientists, or artists, or—"

"Astronauts!" someone in the back yelled.

Everyone started talking at once, making

suggestions and jokes. Caitlin leaped from her chair with her hand waving. Brad called on her.

She took a step forward and gushed, "Rob, I think it's a fantastic idea, and you've really put in a lot of work on it, but"—she turned to face the group—"where are the girls?"

Rob looked confused. "The girls are students from Fort Reno," he said, pointing to his sketch. "They're right here."

Caitlin shook her head and pouted sweetly. "No, I mean *real* girls in beautiful gowns, not cardboard cutouts!"

Realizing what she meant, Brad said dryly, "Caitlin, you'll get your chance to look beautiful on a float. But you'll probably have to wait until homecoming."

Caitlin covered her face with her hands and giggled. "Oh, Brad, stop!" She was pretending to be embarrassed, but when she raised her head, Sara caught a glimmer of triumph in her eyes.

Brad asked if anyone had any other ideas. "If not," he continued, "I think we should go with Rob's!" A resounding cheer came from the group.

Rob took the floor once again and asked for volunteers to help with the design and artwork. Sara summoned her courage and raised her hand high. *At last! Something I know about.*

Brad pointed to her. "Stand up, Sara."

Her heart skipped a beat. He had remembered her name! She carefully placed her purse on her chair and rose to her feet.

Brad grinned. "Everybody, this is Sara, Janie Keating's cousin." There was a loud shuffling of feet and screeching of chairs as they all turned to stare expectantly at her.

Feeling as if a spotlight had suddenly been turned on her, Sara cleared her throat and said shyly, "I've never worked with chicken wire, but—"

Someone from the front yelled, "Speak up!"

A look of surprise crossed her face, and she practically shouted, "I have been working with freestanding sculpture and bas-relief at *der Kunst Institut in Wien.*"

Caitlin laughed sarcastically. "Here in Oklahoma, we usually speak English."

Sara twisted her hands anxiously. "I mean, the Art Institute of Vienna." She giggled nervously and tried to explain herself. "I came here from Austria. Speaking German just comes naturally."

Her eyes darted from face to face. They just stared at her blankly. She looked up at Rob and shrugged. "So I'd like to help with the design—if I could." She sat back down in her chair and stared at her purse in her lap.

Sara could hear Brad talking, but she couldn't bring herself to look at him again. She just sat there wishing the meeting were over. Finally the sound of chairs moving and everyone talking signaled the end. She got up and tried to walk quickly to the door.

"Hey, Sara—wait up!" Rob touched her elbow lightly. "I'd like to know more about this art institute." He held up his sketch pad. "Maybe you can give me some advice on my drawings."

Sara looked into his freckled face, and the knot that had formed in her stomach relaxed. He seemed genuinely interested in her opinion.

"I don't know if I can give you any advice. You're a terrific artist." Sara was surprised to see him blush and it made her like him all the more. "But sure, I'd love to help."

"Why don't you come over to my house tomorrow? We can even get started on the drawings for the float."

"That would be great!" Sara replied. "What time?"

Rob scratched his head. "Let's say, ten o'clock. I'll pick you up at Janie's."

"Terrific!" Sara beamed as they walked

through the gym doors. Rob seemed like a nice guy and she hoped they would be friends.

In the parking lot, kids gathered in groups on the sidewalk, arranging work schedules with each other and waving goodbye.

"Hey," Brad called out. "Anyone need a ride home?"

Sara, feeling good from talking to Rob, started to say that she did. But then Caitlin appeared at Brad's side.

"I'd love a ride, Brad. Why don't we stop for a soda on the way?" She leaned towards him. "My treat!"

"Sounds like a good deal to me," Brad agreed with a laugh.

Sara watched them walk through the parking lot. *Well*, she thought despondently, *I've learned something new about Brad: he's got a car and it seems as if he's got a girlfriend, too.*

At noon the next day Sara and Rob were seated in his kitchen happily munching on tuna fish sandwiches. All morning they had been exchanging ideas about the float and had worked on some more sketches.

"I did that two years ago," Rob said, pointing to a watercolor of a mountain scene over Sara's head. "Isn't it awful?"

Sara eyed it critically, "Well, the perspective is off, but the colors are beautiful."

He set his sandwich down. "My parents insist on framing everything I do."

Sara nodded. It was true. From where she sat she could see into the living room. It seemed that every available wall space had been plastered with a Proctor original.

Rob took a sip of milk and said, "My dad even had me do some paintings for his store."

Sara smiled. "That's great."

Rob have her a deadpan look and drawled, "It's an appliance store. Have you ever tried to paint interesting pictures to complement stoves and refrigerators? It isn't easy!"

Sara started laughing, nearly choking on her sandwich. "My parents haul out all my work every time they have guests over. I stand there looking embarrassed while their friends politely 'ooh' and 'ah' over the worst things. I finally convinced my mom and dad that it was possible for some of my work to be genuinely awful and that some things are better left hidden under the bed."

Rob nodded. "I've discovered the perfect hiding place." He wiped the crumbs off his hands and went into the dining room. As he walked back into the kitchen, he said, "Here are a few of my latest scribblings." He pulled out a large blue watercolor pad and handed it to Sara.

She scooted her chair back and eagerly examined his work. Rob stood a few feet away anxiously studying her face for reactions.

There were some pen-and-ink drawings and a few full-fledged watercolors. "Oh, Rob, some of this is wonderful!"

"And some of it is terrible," he said, pointing to a portrait he had started and then crossed out.

Sara laughed. "I'm not very good at drawing people either. They always end up looking like cartoons."

"All of mine look like me," he said, with a crooked grin, "which is about the same thing."

Sara flipped the page over and a photograph dropped into her lap. It was a picture of a short, round-faced blond girl wearing a fishing vest and proudly holding up a freshly caught trout.

"Is this your girlfriend?"

"You might say that," Rob replied, blushing so furiously that his freckles almost disappeared. "We met at Grand Lake in June when my family went on a camping trip."

He leaned over her shoulder and gazed down at the picture. "Unfortunately Regina lives in Stillwater. We've been writing to each other and talking over the phone, but I don't know when I'll get to see her again."

He cleared his throat and added, "I haven't told anybody about her, because I don't know how it'll work out and, um . . ." His voice trailed off.

Sara handed him the photo and smiled reassuringly. "Don't worry. Your secret is safe with me."

"Thanks," Rob said as he tucked the picture in his shirt pocket.

Sara helped him carry their plates to the sink. She rinsed her glass under the faucet and summoned her courage. "What's Brad Ayres like?" she asked, trying to sound very casual.

"He's a great guy. Why?"

This time it was Sara's turn to blush. "I was just curious. I mean"—she shrugged—"you know."

"Oooh!" Rob's eyes lit up, and he said with a mischievous grin, "You mean what's he *like*?" Sara nodded, embarrassed.

Rob leaned against the sink and said slowly, "Well, he has three brothers, and he's a good student. He plays the guitar, all the kids at school like him. And"—he paused dramatically—"as far as I know, he doesn't have a girlfriend." Rob peered into Sara's face, "Is that what you wanted to know?"

Sara nodded her head briskly and giggled. "Yes."

"Don't worry. I won't tell, if you won't." Rob stuck out his hand.

Sara grasped it and smiled warmly into his freckled face. "It's a deal!" With one quick shake they sealed their newfound friendship.

Chapter Five

"When I open my eyes," Sara said, squeezing her eyelids tight, "he'll be here." She held her breath and counted to thirty, then opened her eyes and looked down at the park. Nothing.

It was a game she had been playing all week. In fact, Sara was becoming obsessed with seeing Brad. She had deliberately signed up to work on the float to be near him, but it hadn't helped at all. She had ended up spending all of her time with Rob on the design, while Brad worked on the construction. Now she found herself taking long walks through town and the park, hoping to catch a glimpse of him.

With a sigh, Sara picked up her journal and placed it on her lap. Her parents had given it to her as a going-away present.

"Be sure and write down all of your first impressions," her mother had told her. "At the end of the year, you'll be surprised at how much you've changed."

She ran her hand across the lavender cloth cover and opened it up to the first page. All it said was, "Oklahoma—Ugh!"

Sara laughed and flipped through the pages. They were covered with doodles in different colors of ink. Occasionally she would get a spurt of writing energy and pour her heart out for pages at a time.

The book flipped open to the place where she had tucked the aerogram she had written to her parents the night before. Sara held it up, reminding herself to mail it on Monday. She started to fold it away, then stopped abruptly. She stared at the street address again. "19 Grunentorgasse." It was their address in Vienna, where her parents were still receiving their mail. It would be forwarded by their neighbor, who had their itinerary. Sara had been there just a short while before, but already her German was starting to slip. The once familiar words looked foreign. She translated it out loud: "19 Green-door-alley."

Sara thought about the letter. She had tried to be cheery and positive in all of her letters to her parents. She didn't want them to worry about her, but sometimes she missed them so much.

She slipped the letter back into her book. On the open page, she'd written, "I feel so alone here, like a complete stranger in my own country. When will I ever fit in?" At the bottom she had drawn a heart with Brad's name inside.

The next few pages were covered with "Brad and Sara" and "Sara and Brad," written in different colors of ink and in Sara's best calligraphy. A sketch of his face covered the entire next page. It was a pretty good likeness, and Sara smiled when she thought of how much care she had taken in drawing his curly, sun-streaked hair. She was certain it must be soft. Sara wistfully brushed a lock of her own hair off her forehead. She imagined herself running her fingers through Brad's curls.

Sara cocked her head and critically studied her sketch. She hadn't gotten the eyes quite right. The laughter in them wasn't there. She reached for her pencil, which was lying in its case a few feet away.

A zing like an electrical current shot through her, and Sara pulled her hand back with a startled cry.

There, just inches away from her fingers,

was a pair of loafers attached to a pair of jean-clad legs, attached to a tall, lean body. She tilted her head up and looked straight into Brad's face.

Brad took a quick step back and said, "Sorry. I didn't mean to scare you." He shoved his hands into his pockets. "I saw you sitting up here and I—uh—I wanted to say hello. But"—he gestured with his elbow toward her journal—"you seemed to be studying so hard that I didn't want to disturb you."

Sara jerked her head back to look at her journal. There staring up at her was his picture. She quickly slammed the cover shut. Panic filled her as she realized that he might have seen the picture. She glared intensely at his face, looking for signs that he had.

Her stare made Brad uncomfortable, and he backed away even more. "I didn't want to interrupt, I just wanted to say hi!"

Finally Sara managed to say, "You aren't interrupting. Honest. I was just writing in my journal." She quickly tossed it onto the grass, feeling as though it were poison. She secretly vowed never to take it out of her room again!

"Oh, you keep a diary?" Brad asked, kneeling down beside her.

"Yes. I mean, no." Her head was beginning

to ache with confusion. "I mean, I've just started it recently."

"I've been keeping one for a couple of years," Brad said, tugging at a blade of grass. "They're pretty good for sorting things out sometimes."

Sara eyed the book, which was lying a few feet away from her. All Brad would have to do was pick it up and if it fell open, he'd know!

"Of course," Brad continued, "I have to be careful where I hide it. My younger brothers are pretty big snoops, and they love to tease me."

That was all Sara needed to hear. She grabbed the book and clutched it to her chest. "My mother suggested I keep one to write down my feelings about America."

"Well, how do you like it so far?" he asked.

"It's OK. I mean, it's fine." She wanted to kick herself for sounding so scatter-brained. But she couldn't shake the feeling that he had X-ray eyes and knew exactly what she was holding. She took a deep breath and said, "It's just—different. I'm still trying to adjust."

He nodded sympathetically at her, and she quickly looked down at the ground. She tried desperately to think of something else to say, but her mind had gone blank. There he was, sitting right next to her, and she couldn't even look at him!

They sat there for what seemed like an eternity of uncomfortable silence. Brad kept pulling at blades of grass while Sara tapped her sandaled feet together. Her mind kept screaming, *Say something, stupid!* but her mouth was paralyzed.

"Well," Brad said, brushing the grass from his jeans, "I just wanted to thank you for your help." He stood up. "On the float, I mean. You and Rob are doing a great job." He started backing away from her.

Sara leaped to her feet. She wanted to tell him to wait, but she could only stammer, "Thanks. It's been a lot of fun. Rob's a great guy!"

A funny look crossed Brad's face as he said, "He sure is. You two make a good team." Then he added brusquely, "I've got to run. I'll see you later."

"Bye, Brad," Sara called in a quiet little voice as she watched him saunter down the hill.

She angrily hit her head with her journal. *I've been waiting all week for this moment, and I blew it! Why didn't I ask him about himself? There are a million things we could have talked about.*

She watched Brad stride across the park, the warm wind whipping his shirt against his body. At the tennis courts, Brad turned the corner and disappeared out of sight.

Sara squeezed her eyes tight again and whispered intensely, "When I open my eyes, he'll come back." She held her breath for a whole minute and then opened her blue eyes wide. Nothing. Just the sun beating down on the park below.

That night, as Janie and Sara were getting ready for bed, Sara turned to Janie. "Do you think I'm pretty?" she asked.

Janie, who had her football jersey nightshirt halfway over her head, mumbled, "What?"

Sara perched at the head of her bed with her knees tucked under her chin and said, "No, I mean, really."

"I can't believe you're asking me this," Janie said as she tugged her nightshirt down. "You're beautiful. You look like a ballerina."

"I don't feel like a dancer. I'm so klutzy."

"All the girls wish they looked like you," Janie argued. She picked up her brush and ran it quickly through her hair.

"I'm not talking about girls." Sara rested her cheek on her hands. "I mean guys. Do you think they think I'm—attractive?"

"I think you must have been living on Mars for the last sixteen years." Janie walked over to the bed and pounded her pillow. "Of course they think you're attractive."

"Then why won't any of them talk to me?" Sara asked, raising her head.

Janie sat cross-legged on her bed and eyed her cousin seriously. "Well, maybe it's because you seem sort of—sort of aloof."

"Aloof?" Sara asked, feeling a little bewildered.

Janie nodded. "Maybe they're afraid of you. You do act awfully sophisticated."

Sara stretched her legs out in front of her. "I'm not sophisticated, I'm a bowl of mush. I can never think of the right thing to say, so I guess I just clam up."

Janie flopped on her back. "I'm the complete opposite. I always open my big mouth before I think."

"But you're so bubbly and funny, people can't help liking you."

"Yeah, and they treat me like I'm an airhead."

"What? They do not."

Janie protested, "No, it's true! If I ever bothered to count how many times people patted me on the head and said 'Oh, Janie!' I'd be too depressed to ever leave the house."

Sara laughed and found herself saying, "Oh, Janie!"

Janie threw her pillow at Sara and wailed, "See?"

Sara caught the pillow and hugged it, laughing, "I can't help it! You are genuinely funny!"

"Just once I'd like to be taken seriously." Janie yawned and pulled back her covers.

Sara turned on her stomach, looking at her pillow. "When my mom and dad said I would be moving here, I thought it would be a great opportunity to change. You know, become a whole new person." She smoothed the pillowcase. "I've always been shy, and making new friends is just so hard for me. For some reason I thought that when I got off the plane, I'd suddenly be carefree and outgoing," she said with a halfhearted laugh. Turning on her back, she added, "The only problem is, when I landed, I was just the same old me."

"You think too much," Janie said as she reached over for her pillow. "Don't be so hard on yourself. Even the most outgoing person in the world has a tough time in a new place."

Sara climbed under the covers and said with a sigh, "Yeah, I guess you're right."

"You just need to loosen up a little," Janie mumbled as she stuck the pillow under her head. "Give people a chance to get to know you."

Sara switched off the bedside light. She lay there in the darkness, pondering Janie's words and listening to the house shift and creak as it settled. Upstairs the refrigerator motor kicked on, humming noisily through the stillness.

Finally Sara took a deep breath and said quietly, "I guess what I'm really worried about is not just people in general, but Brad. How do I get him to like me?" She folded her hands across the covers and stared up at the ceiling. "I think he kind of likes me, but then again, I think he likes everybody." She sighed. "He sure is handsome. Not rugged-handsome like Judd, but sensitive-handsome. Sometimes when he looks at me I feel as if he's looking right into my soul. That sounds silly, doesn't it? But there's a look that comes into his eyes. It's a kind of sparkle that says 'Life isn't as bad as it seems sometimes.' " Sara turned her head towards Janie's bed, "Have you ever noticed it? Janie? Janie?" she whispered. "Are you asleep?"

Sara listened to the soft snore coming from Janie's bed. She dropped back on her pillow with a small chuckle. Janie hadn't heard a word of her heartfelt confession.

"I guess my secret's still safe," she said out loud to the darkness. Somewhere off in the distance. a dog barked. Boxcars creaked and rattled their way across the Rock Island train trestle. She closed her eyes and let the slow clicking of the rails lull her to sleep.

Chapter Six

"Keep down!" Janie whispered as they drove into the parking lot at Brisco High.

Sara wound herself into a tight ball, trying to hide. Her heart was beating fast, and she wondered for the millionth time what she was doing there.

Janie had insisted that the only way for Sara to get to know people was if she joined in group activities. The prank at Brisco High was the first thing that had come up. It seemed like a fun idea when Janie told her about it, but now the fear of getting caught was too much for Sara to bear. And when she heard the sound of another car, Sara squeezed her arms tighter around her knees.

Janie turned off the engine and pulled on the emergency brake. "It's OK," she whispered, tapping Sara on the shoulder. "It's only Caroline."

Sara peeked over the dashboard and watched a red convertible pull alongside them. Both cars cut their lights.

Suzanna, who had ducked down in the backseat, raised her head and rasped, "Why are we whispering?"

Janie turned in her seat. "Someone might hear us, that's why."

Suzanna sat up straight in the back and asked in a normal voice, "Who? There's not a house or another car in sight."

Sara stared out at the empty road, watching for lights. Suzanna was right. Brisco High sat in the middle of a field on the outskirts of town. No lights were on at the school, and the deserted buildings loomed ominously in the dark.

There was a loud *thunk* as Caroline got out of her car and slammed the door shut. Sara watched Caitlin stand up in her seat and vault lightly over the side of the convertible. When she landed she announced, "The 'Cavalry' has arrived!"

At the same time Caroline opened the trunk and pulled out a large cardboard box and two flashlights.

"Did you get it?" Janie called out as she stepped onto the gravel.

"Yeah," Caroline answered, shining her light at their car. "It was in an old trunk in the attic."

Sara and Suzanna reached for their flashlights and leaped out of the car. They all moved toward the school lawn, where Caroline set the box down. They aimed their flashlights on it.

"My dad wore this to a Halloween party a long time ago," Caroline said as she bent over the box. "I didn't get a chance to really look at it. I hope it's not full of moth holes."

She pulled out a large blue jacket and a pair of trousers. They were made of felt with gold epaulets on the shoulders and gold stripes down the pant legs.

"Did he say you could take it?" Sara asked innocently.

"No, but he won't mind. That trunk hasn't been opened in years." She held the cavalry uniform up to her body. "He'll never miss it."

Caitlin laughed and said, "Oh, honey, it's you."

Caroline was a tall, heavy girl, and the pants were at least three times too big for her. *Her father must be huge!* Sara thought.

Caroline plopped the hat on her head, and

it fell down over her eyes. That set everyone giggling.

"*Shh,*" Suzanna said. "Come on, we've got to hurry before the guys get here with their costume!"

"They're just going to die when they discover we got here first and ruined their plans," Caitlin said.

Caroline carried the box, and they all scurried up the sidewalk. As they got closer to the school, some headlights came over the crest of the hill. "Hit the dirt!" Janie bellowed.

They all turned and looked before diving onto the grass. No one even dared to take a breath until the car on the road sped past and disappeared out of sight.

"Is everybody OK?" Caroline asked, pulling her red baseball cap back on her head. Although there were a couple of nervous giggles as they groped for their flashlights, no one seemed to be injured. When they found their flashlights, the girls shone them on one another for the first time since they'd arrived.

Caitlin screeched as her light hit Sara. "What have you got on your face!"

"Well, it's—" Sara said as her hand flew to the charcoal she had smeared on her cheeks and forehead.

"Camouflage, of course," Janie answered.

She pointed to Caitlin. "*You* were the one who said we should all wear black."

"Black *clothes*, not war paint," Caitlin replied, flicking her light over their faces. "You look ridiculous."

"Well, this isn't a fashion show, you know," Suzanna said defensively.

Sara directed her light on Caitlin. She was wearing a black, shiny leotard top with charcoal jeans. She had tied a black scarf around her neck, and it made her look as if she had just stepped out of a James Bond movie.

How does Caitlin do it? Sara wondered, gazing down at her own baggy black sweat pants and torn navy blue T-shirt. She was sure everyone would have laughed at her if she had dressed the way Caitlin had.

Caroline picked up the box. "I don't know about you guys, but I've got a job to do."

They all followed her up the walk and stopped in front of a large statue of an Indian.

"Are they the Brisco Indians?" Sara asked.

That time everyone turned their flashlights on her, causing Sara to squint and step back.

"Well, of course!" they all yelled at once.

"Where have you been all your life?" Caitlin asked, sounding truly shocked that Sara had even dared ask such a question.

Sara stepped back and mumbled, "Sorry. I didn't know."

Janie was standing facing the statue, and she tilted her head back to look up at it. "It's bigger than I'd remembered. We should have brought a ladder."

"No problem!" Caroline said. "We can make a pyramid and reach it that way."

They all put their flashlights down and lined up next to one another. Caitlin took charge. "Now, the big girls should be on the bottom. That means Caroline and Sara."

Sara resented being called "big," but went along with it anyway. She and Caroline got down on their hands and knees, their shoulders together.

"Now. Janie, you stand on their backs, and I'll get on your shoulders, since I'm the smallest."

"What should I do?" Suzanna asked.

"You hand me the uniform so I can dress him and make sure I don't fall!"

Janie climbed onto Sara and Caroline and braced her hands against the statue.

"Janie Keating, I think you must have put on a few pounds," Caroline called out.

Janie laughed and lightly tapped Caroline on the head. "I have not!"

Then Caitlin bounced onto Janie's shoulders, and Janie let out a scream. "Now I have!" She struggled to keep her balance. "About one hundred and five pounds."

That started Caroline and Sara giggling, and the whole pyramid threatened to collapse.

"Stop laughing!" Caitlin ordered, gripping the statue around the neck. "Suzanna, hand me the jacket," she called. Grabbing the jacket from Suzanna, she draped it over the Indian's shoulders and then yelled down for the pants.

Caroline turned her head to Suzanna and said, "There's some rope in the box. Thread it through the belt loops and Caitlin can tie it around his waist."

"And hurry! I think my elbows are going to give out!" Sara added.

The whole group swayed as Caitlin stretched her arms around the statue's waist and tied a knot in the rope.

Caroline moaned, "I don't think I can hold out much longer!"

Suzanna hurriedly dug in the box and pulled out the hat. Janie, keeping her eyes forward, carefully reached out one hand to take it. She wobbled a little, grasped the hat and then slowly raised her arm.

Just as Caitlin was placing it on the statue's head, a loud male voice boomed, "Don't anybody move!"

All the girls screamed at once, and the pyramid teetered to the right and collapsed in slow motion. Sara and Caroline landed on their stomachs flat on the grass with a loud "Oomph." Caitlin struggled to grab the statue and then leaped backward off Janie's shoulders. Janie fell on her knees between Caroline and Sara.

No one was hurt, but all their hearts were pounding as four flashlights blinded them.

Then a loud burst of laughter came from behind the lights, and they realized who it was.

"Rob Proctor," Suzanna screamed. "I could just strangle you!" Then Suzanna chased him down the front lawn, swatting at him.

"You scared the daylights out of me!" Caitlin yelled, running after Rob as well.

"That was the idea!" someone else called out.

"That sounds like you, Judd Parkin!" Janie said.

Another voice answered, "You got it!"

Caroline gasped. "And Peter Silbert!"

She and Janie bounced to their feet. "Get them," they yelled.

They charged after the two boys. "Look out!"

Judd and Peter hollered as they raced off in different directions.

Sara pulled herself up and was immediately seized with a fit of giggling as she watched her friends run back and forth across the lawn, trying to catch the boys.

One boy was still standing in front of her. He was laughing, too. Sara gripped her stomach, trying to catch her breath. "I thought I'd die of a heart attack," she gasped.

"I wish I'd had a camera," the boy said with a laugh. "You looked so funny."

Sara recognized Brad's voice, and her eyes widened. For a brief moment she started to freeze up, but the whole situation was so ridiculous that she started giggling all over again. Together they watched as Suzanna and Caitlin tackled Rob.

Sara finally stopped laughing. "How did you know we were here, anyway?"

"We drove past on the highway and saw you girls running up to the front of the school," Brad replied matter-of-factly.

"You recognized us?" Sara asked, surprised. "Even in our disguises?"

"How could anyone miss you?" he replied. "You turned around and looked, right out there on the sidewalk, as plain as day."

Brad shone his flashlight on Sara's face,

and she suddenly remembered the charcoal. Brad burst out laughing, and she covered her face with her hands.

"It was Janie's idea," she protested through her fingers. "I think she saw it in a war movie or something."

"Well," Brad said, chuckling, "if you've made any plans to become a spy—"

"I'd better give them up," Sara finished for him.

"Right," Brad said as he reached out in the darkness and lightly touched her arm.

His hand lingered there for a moment and sent a tingle through Sara's entire body. She couldn't see his face, but she knew he had to be smiling.

At that moment, Caitlin and Suzanna reappeared, dragging Rob by the elbows.

"OK, OK, I give up!" Rob yelled. "Brad! Sara! Help me! They're going to tickle me to death!"

Caitlin whirled around to face Brad. "Make one move and you'll get the same treatment."

Brad took a few steps backward. "Rob, you're a good friend, but you're on your own this time!"

Suzanna and Caitlin then pounced on Rob again. Suzanna shouted, "Laugh, you rat! Laugh!"

"I'll remember this, Brad!" Rob called,

clutching his sides and trying to sound fierce. But he was laughing so hard that he didn't sound threatening at all. Soon, Caroline and Janie arrived from different directions, with Judd and Peter in tow. They were both shouting protests all the way.

As they stumbled back to the lawn where the others were, Janie wrapped her arms around Judd's waist. He stumbled forward in his cowboy boots, dragging Janie behind him.

"This girl is like glue. Somebody get her off of me!" Judd shouted. But he didn't seem to be struggling very hard. Sara grinned, knowing that Janie was enjoying every minute of it.

Another light flashed over the horizon, and they all threw themselves to the ground.

Brad whispered from the grass near Sara, "We'd better get out of here. Anyone can see us."

Everyone mumbled in agreement and hastily grabbed their flashlights and belongings.

As they headed toward the cars, Judd remembered that he had parked his car down the road and would have to walk all the way to it. "Can we—uh—catch a ride to my car with you guys?" he asked.

"No way!" Caitlin said, putting her hands

on her hips. "This is your punishment for scaring us half to death!"

The guys all shuffled their feet, mumbling to each other. "Aw, come on!!" Judd said, facing the girls.

"Pretty please!" Rob begged. He dropped down to one knee and clasped his hands together.

Caitlin turned triumphantly to the other girls. "What do you think? Should we help these poor unfortunate boys so they don't have to walk *all* that way?"

The girls were enjoying their power and took their time coming to a decision.

"What'll you give us?" Janie asked coquettishly.

"Our undying devotion," Brad replied.

Suzanna snorted. "I'll remember that next time I need a date."

"Oh, all right. We'll give you a ride," Caroline finally said.

Brad was standing next to Sara, their shoulders almost touching. She grinned boldly at him in the darkness. She couldn't wait to sit next to him in the car.

They had started to walk toward the station wagon when Caitlin stopped them. "Wait a minute! Rob and Sara should ride together," she called out. She skipped over toward Sara and whispered in an extra-loud voice, "You make such a cute couple."

There was an awkward pause, and Sara didn't know what to say. She shrugged helplessly toward Brad.

Rob gallantly tried to help out. "Aw, come on," he said, "I want to ride in the convertible." He ran his hand through his wiry red hair. "I like to feel the wind in my face."

Caitlin ignored Rob's comment. "Judd, you ride with them." She hooked her arm in Brad's and purred, "And Brad and Peter will ride with us." Sara watched Caitlin lean her head against Brad's shoulder. "OK?"

Brad looked quickly at Sara and then back at Caitlin. Sara held her breath, hoping he'd say no, but he just shrugged. "Sure. That's fine with me."

Sara watched them move toward the convertible feeling like a deflated balloon. With a sigh, she opened the car door and slid in next to Rob and Suzanna. Before the overhead light went off, Rob gave her an apologetic look. She smiled and mouthed, "Thanks."

"My keys!" Janie screeched from the front seat. "I can't find them!"

"Did you look in your purse!" Suzanna asked helpfully.

"Check the glove compartment," Rob added.

Judd, who was sitting in front with Janie, ducked his head under the dashboard. "Maybe you tossed them under the seat."

"Janie Keating," Suzanna warned, "if you make me crawl around on the grass in the dark, I'll never forgive you!"

"Now, don't panic," Janie said, nervously checking behind the visor. "I know they're here someplace."

Rob and Suzanna leaned forward and groped around the floor of the backseat. Janie and Judd were checking through the assortment of maps and gum wrappers in the glove compartment. Quietly Sara asked, "Janie, did you check the ignition?"

Everyone froze, waiting for her answer. Slowly she turned and faced the wheel.

"Well, what do you know?" she chirped brightly. "Here they are!"

Rob and Suzanna sat up abruptly. "Janie Keating!" they both yelled.

Janie started the engine and turned to face Judd, who was staring at her, openmouthed. "Everybody ready?" She jerked the car into drive and bounced up onto the curb.

"*Reverse!*" everyone bellowed. They bumped backward off the curb, stopped, then lurched forward out of the parking lot.

"Janie Keating, you keep your mind on the

road," Suzanna instructed, leaning over the seat.

Sara nodded vigorously. "I'm glad I'm not the only one who worries about that."

"Don't worry," Judd said with a grin, moving closer to Janie. "I'll keep a close eye on her!" Janie giggled wildly, and her foot accidentally pushed down harder on the gas pedal. They accelerated onto the road, knocking Rob back between Sara and Suzanna.

Rob grinned crookedly. "How about this? Two girls for every boy!" He draped his gangly arms over their shoulders. "Now that's the way it should be!"

Sara turned, wiggling her fingers, and said, "You better watch out, 'Doctor Proctor,' or we'll"—she winked at Suzanna and they finished the sentence in unison—"tickle you to death."

The girls dug their fingers into his ribs, and as the station wagon sped down the highway, Rob shrieked, "Help! Uncle!"

Chapter Seven

The next Tuesday Sara trudged wearily up the front steps. Her arms ached from working on the plastering for the float. All she wanted to do was take a shower and fall asleep. As she passed the mirror in the front hall, she did a double take. Little bits of white plaster were caked in her hair and on her cheeks, and one of her braids was coming undone.

How long have I looked like this? she wondered as she licked her finger and wiped off the plaster. *No wonder I don't have a date for the dance!*

She could hear her aunt Dorsie and grandmother having a heated argument in the kitchen. "You're all wrong," her grandmother said, slamming something on the table. "Francine left Sean because she found out he was her half brother."

"He was never her brother," Dorsie interrupted. "He was her step-father. It happened just after her mother's second marriage to Phil. Don't you remember? Phil left Edith and she married Sean shortly after that. But it was always kept a secret."

"Oh, that's right," Sara's grandmother said. "And Sean is the father of Francine's half brother, Tom."

Sara's eyes widened, and she quietly set her purse on the couch and tiptoed to the kitchen door. She held her breath and listened.

"I always get Tom and Sean confused," Sara's grandmother said, opening the refrigerator door.

Sara leaned against the wall, amazed at what she was hearing.

Her aunt clanged the lid over a pot on the stove. "That's because they both look so young. But you know," she added, lowering her voice as Sara craned her neck to listen, "Sean is really forty-five. He had his face rebuilt and assumed a whole new identity after that hideous fire in Milwaukee. His name is actually Wilfred Crane, and that's what it was when he was married to Edith."

"You're kidding!" Sara and her grandmother both blurted out simultaneously.

Sara clapped her hand over her mouth, hoping they hadn't heard her, but it was too late.

"Sara, is that you?" her grandmother called from the kitchen.

"Yeah, I just got home!" Sara said, trying to sound nonchalant. She walked casually over to the table, dying of curiosity.

"How's the float coming?" Sara's grandmother asked as she set a stack of four plates on the table.

"The float's fine," Sara hurriedly replied, putting a plate in front of each chair. She didn't want to talk about the float. She was too worried about Francine and Edith and Sean, whoever they were. She stared expectantly at her grandmother and aunt, who were bustling around the kitchen.

Finally she couldn't stand the suspense any longer. "What's going to happen to Francine?" she blurted out.

Her aunt paused and turned toward Sara, holding a strawberry-shaped potholder in midair. "We won't find out until Friday."

Her grandmother nodded in agreement. "They always save the juicy stuff till Friday so you'll be sure and tune in again on Monday."

Sara took a step backward and looked from her grandmother to her aunt. "Tune in?" She couldn't believe what she was hearing. "You were talking about a TV show?!"

"Well, of course! It's our favorite soap opera," her aunt Dorsie said, reaching into the oven.

At that moment the back door swung open, and Janie charged into the room.

"He asked me! Judd actually asked me to the dance!" She bounced from her grandmother to her mother, hugging them both. Her mother nearly dropped the potpies she was balancing on a cookie sheet, and her grandmother held the milk carton away from her to keep from spilling it.

Sara hugged Janie, too. "That's terrific!" she cried. The two of them hopped up and down, squealing.

"Who's Judd?" their grandmother shouted over the din.

Janie's jaw fell open. "Who's Judd! He's only the most gorgeous fullback at Fort Reno High!" She ran over to her grandmother and threw her arms around her neck. "And he's taking me to the dance!"

Finally her mother gestured for everyone to sit down. "Eat before your food gets cold. I'm not sure they're cooked through anyway." She stuck her finger into one of the pies and quickly withdrew it. "Ouch!" she exclaimed, shaking her hand. "They're done! Now sit down."

Janie and Sara scooted into their chairs, chatting excitedly.

"How did he ask you?" Sara questioned, putting her napkin in her lap.

"Well, you know he's on the dance committee," Janie began, taking a quick sip of her milk. "Caroline told him we needed some strong men to help out, so he signed up. I could just kiss Caroline." She dug into her chicken potpie and blew on her fork. "Anyway, we worked it so he and I would be in charge of finding the kites."

"Why do you need kites for a dance?" her mother asked, interrupting. "I thought it was indoors."

Janie rolled her eyes at Sara. "They're part of the decorations, Mom!"

"I was just asking!" her mother said, reaching for the salt.

"So, for the past few days Judd and I have been driving around Oklahoma City together looking for kites."

"I didn't know you were in the city." Her mother interrupted again.

"Yes, you did. I told you. You must have

forgotten." Janie heaved a big sigh. "*Anyway*, today when he dropped me off, I asked him."

Sara was shocked. "*You* asked *him*?" she cried.

"Well, sort of. I mean, I asked him who he was going with, and he said nobody. So then I told him it was our duty as members of the dance committee to be there to make sure everything goes well."

"What did he say when you said that?" Sara asked, wide-eyed.

Janie shrugged. "He agreed with me and suggested that maybe we should go together— since we're on the committee and all."

"Is that when you said yes?" her grand-mother asked.

"Are you kidding!" Janie replied indignantly. "I didn't want him to think that I didn't have a date." She grinned impishly. "I told him that I had already made a commitment, but that I could probably get out of it and I'd let him know tonight."

Sara shook her head in amazement at Ja-nie. She wished she had that kind of nerve.

"You tricked him into it!" her grandmother objected.

Janie looked shocked. "I did not! I just gave him a little nudge." She tossed her head knowingly. "Guys don't know what they want, and it's our duty as women to tell them."

Her mother pointed her fork at her. "Janie Keating, sometimes I worry about you."

Janie rolled her eyes again. "Oh, Mother!"

"So, Sara, who's taking you to the dance?" her grandmother asked, reaching for a piece of bread.

Sara's mouth was full, but she managed to mumble, "Nobody." Then she swallowed and added with a small laugh, "It looks like I'll be sitting this one out."

Janie dropped her fork and said, "I thought you'd be going with Rob."

Sara gave her a confused look. "Why Rob?"

"Well, you two have been spending so much time together. I thought you liked each other."

"That's just because we're working on the float."

Janie cocked her head and shrugged. "All I know is, everyone thinks you're a couple."

Sara was appalled and stared at Janie in shock. "Everyone thinks that? That's awful!" Then she quickly added, "I mean, I like Rob a lot, but there is absolutely nothing romantic going on at all."

"Is Rob that redheaded kid who picks you up every morning?" her aunt Dorsie asked.

Sara was still staring at Janie. "How could

anyone think that? All we do is work night and day on that stupid float!"

Their grandmother shook her head. "I think he's good-looking. He's tall and thin with that nice thick red hair."

"Those freckles make him look goofy," her daughter argued.

"He's not goofy-looking," Sara said impatiently. "And, anyway, it doesn't matter what he looks like. We're just good friends, and we're not going to the dance together."

"Well," her grandmother said reassuringly, "I bet lots of kids will be there without dates. Why don't you go anyway?"

"Sure!" Sara's aunt chimed in. "Gran and I will drive you over."

"Oh, Sara, come on. It'll be lots of fun," Janie agreed enthusiastically.

"No!" Sara yelled, horrified at the thought of being dropped off at a dance by her grandmother and aunt. She wasn't all that crazy about going without a date, either.

The determined look on Sara's face surprised everyone, and they all turned their attention to their dinner in silence.

Finally, Sara's grandmother spoke up. "There must be lots of nice boys who don't have dates," she said. She looked at her daughter.

"Doesn't Mrs. Kincaid have a son in high school?"

"Yes," her daughter replied. "Mark. I'll call her and see if he's going."

Janie set her glass down with a loud clunk. "Mother! Mark is thirteen years old!" The humiliation was becoming too much to bear. "The only guy I'd like to go to the dance with is Brad, and he's already taken," Sara cried.

Janie turned around to face Sara. "Brad?" Surprise covered her face, and then she hit her head with her hand. "Of course! You guys would be perfect together!"

"Who's Brad?" The older women both asked at the same time.

"I didn't know you liked Brad!" Janie continued, ignoring their question.

Sara immediately regretted mentioning Brad's name, and she tried to sluff it off. "Well I do like him, but he and Caitlin seem to be a couple."

"He's not going with Caitlin."

Sara perked up. "What?"

"Haven't you heard? Caitlin has a date with a guy from the University of Oklahoma. He's in her brother's fraternity. That's all she's been talking about for the last three days." Janie smiled mischievously and practically sang out, "I don't think Brad is going with anyone."

Sara's head was spinning. She felt her heart start pounding as she thought about the possibility of going to the dance with Brad.

"Call him up!" Aunt Dorsie ordered.

Sara gave her a horrified look. "I can't call him, I've hardly even spoken to him! And I always say the stupidest things in front of him." Sara pushed her plate away from her place. "He must think I'm a big zero."

"That's not true," Janie said. "Last Thursday night at Brisco, you two seemed to be getting along fine."

Sara felt another surge of hope. They had had fun together, and there had been something special about the look he had given her just before Caitlin dragged him off.

"What about Brisco?" Janie's mother asked. "I'm certain you didn't tell me you went there."

Janie gave her mother a stern look. "We're not talking about Brisco, we're talking about Brad and Sara and getting them together."

"This all sounds like one of your soap operas," Sara said dejectedly.

Janie held her fork up like a microphone and said in her deepest voice, "Will Sara and Brad go to the dance and find true happiness? Tune in Friday and see."

Chapter Eight

The next day Rob and Sara were bent over a bucket of plaster and warm water, trying to finish the uniform for General Sheridan. It was a process that Rob called "Dip and Drape." Sara and Rob dipped the clothes, and then draped them over the statue, positioning them the way they wanted the clothes to hang when they hardened. Earlier that morning they had soaked trousers in the plaster mixture, and they were already drying on the statue.

"Knock! Knock!" Caitlin called, sticking her head around the door of the art room.

"Come in," Sara and Rob both called without lifting their heads.

"Hi, you guys. I just stopped in to see how things were going."

"We're a little behind schedule," Rob said,

wiping some plaster off his forehead with the back of his hand. "But other than that, everything's OK." As he wiped his forehead, he left a clump of white plaster in his wiry red hair.

Sara dipped the coat she was holding into the plaster. Then she and Rob carefully walked with it toward the plaster sculpture.

Caitlin scooted out of their way. "Oooh, what's that?" she squealed.

"General Sheridan's coat," Rob murmured, trying to keep it from dripping on him. "We finished the body yesterday, and now we're trying to put some clothes on the poor guy."

Caitlin watched them move toward the white figure propped against the wall. "He looks like a mummy!"

"In a way he is," Sara said, sliding the right sleeve over the plaster arm. "Peter Silbert volunteered to let us cover him in gauze and plaster to make the model. It was sort of like putting him in a full body cast."

Caitlin gasped. "He's not still in there, is he?"

"I hope not!" Rob said in mock horror. He leaned his head toward the chest and called, "Peter, are you in there? Speak to me, Peter!"

Caitlin put her hands on her hips. "You're just kidding me!"

Sara slipped the other sleeve over General Sheridan and explained, "We only did half of him at a time, so he was never really completely wrapped up. But it's a pretty complicated process."

"Poor Pete didn't know what he was getting himself into," Rob said, laughing. "We had to cover his face in petroleum jelly, and he looked pretty funny."

Sara joined in. "And with those straws sticking out of his nose, he looked *very* funny."

"Sounds like torture to me," Caitlin said, wrinkling her nose.

"I'm sure Peter would agree with you," Rob said.

Sara very carefully smoothed the jacket, then stepped back. "It looks pretty good, doesn't it?"

Rob cocked his head, eyeing the general critically. "Well, right now it looks like Peter Silbert in a wet jacket, but once it dries and we put the beard on him, he'll look terrific."

Caitlin hopped onto one of the wooden stools near their worktable and sighed. "All that artsy stuff is beyond me. I could never do it." She looked directly at Sara. "It's so messy."

Sara wiped her hands on her plaster- and paint-smeared lab coat. "Then I guess it's a good thing your job is stuffing napkins in chicken wire."

"Oh, that's so boring," Caitlin said with a pert toss of her head. "Besides, it's practically finished. That's why I gave up and decided to see how you were doing." She folded her arms across her chest. "Well, Sara, what lucky guy is taking you to the dance?"

Sara was too embarrassed to admit that she didn't have a date, so she stammered, "I can't go. I've got too much work to do. The float and all . . ." She gestured helplessly around her.

Rob came to the rescue. "Sara volunteered to put the finishing touches on the float so that the rest of us could go to the dance. I think it was really nice of her to offer."

Sara turned to the nearest art table and shuffled some sketches, her face flushing. She tried desperately to think of some witty remark to show that it didn't matter.

"Gee, Sara," Caitlin said sweetly, "we'll all miss you." She hopped off her stool and bounced toward the door. "It's all going to be so much fun. Listen, I'll see you guys later, OK?" She paused at the door and waved.

"Keep up the good work!"

The glass in the upper half of the door rattled as Caitlin shut it behind her. Rob and

Sara listened to her footsteps fade away down the hall.

Sara, still staring at the table, bit her lip. "Thanks, Rob," she said quietly.

Rob pulled a stool up next to Sara. "Don't let her get to you."

Sara slammed her fist against the table. "I can't help it!" She looked into Rob's face. "Why doesn't she like me?"

"Well," Rob said, running his hand through his hair, "she's obviously jealous of you."

"Me? Why on earth would she be jealous of me?" Sara asked, standing up and pacing around the room.

"Because you're everything she's not. You're beautiful, talented, traveled, and tall."

Sara scrunched her nose. "Oh, I am not."

"Yes, you are. And Caitlin's cute, perky, popular, and short."

"Petite," Sara corrected him, still pacing.

"Excuse me," Rob said, grinning. "Petite." He leaned back with his elbows on the table. "But I left out the most important factor."

Sara stopped and turned to face him. "What?"

"Brad."

Sara took a frustrated swipe at Rob.

"It's true!" Rob protested. "I've seen the way he watches you, and so has Caitlin. Haven't you noticed that if Brad says so much as 'hello' to you, she's right there?"

"I thought I was just imagining it," Sara replied. "Wait a minute! Why would she be upset? She's going with someone else to the dance."

This was news to Rob, and he perked up. "What? I hadn't heard that. Who?"

"You and I have spent so much time with our heads in this plaster that we seem to be the last to know." She leaned forward and rested her elbows on the table. "Janie told me that Caitlin has a hot date with some guy in her brother's college fraternity."

Rob raised his eyebrows. "Oh, a college man!"

Sara shrugged. "I guess so."

"Talk about a change of heart," Rob said, shaking his head. He checked over his shoulder to make sure Caitlin hadn't come back and lowered his voice. "The way I heard it, Caitlin was determined to go to the dance with Brad. That was the only reason she signed up to work on the float."

Sara was shocked. "You're kidding!" That was her reason, too, but she didn't want to mention it.

"You heard her say how boring it was. That horse is the farthest thing from her mind."

"If she likes Brad so much," Sara asked, knitting her brow, "then why isn't she going to the dance with him?"

Rob folded his arms across his chest and looked at Sara. "Maybe he didn't ask her."

It hadn't occurred to Sara that Brad wouldn't have asked Caitlin. She started pacing again. After she had circled the table twice, Rob stopped her. "Will you stand still? I'm getting dizzy!"

Sara stood still and began twisting her long braid. "I'm trying to sort things out. Now, if Caitlin wanted to go with Brad, but he didn't ask her, and she got her brother to get her a date, then who's Brad going with?"

Rob looked confused.

"What I mean is"—she threw her arms up in despair—"why hasn't he asked me?"

Rob dropped his hands into his lap and shrugged. "That, I can't figure out." He looked up at the ceiling and then back at Sara. "Maybe he thinks you don't like him."

"What?" Sara exclaimed, flabbergasted. All she ever thought about was Brad. She felt like she was wearing a neon sign that flashed his name whenever he appeared.

"Maybe you need to let him know that you like him. Try a few of Caitlin's tactics."

Sara fluttered her eyelids at Rob and spoke

in a syrupy voice. "Brad, honey, I'm crazy about you! If you feel the same way I'd just love it if you'd escort me to the dance on Friday."

Rob raised one eyebrow. "Not quite like that, but close."

"I could never do that!" Sara said, wrinkling her nose.

"You're right." Rob laughed. "Well, I guess you'll just have to be your own sweet self and snare him that way."

"Oh, boy," Sara said lifelessly.

"Speaking of sweet, wonderful girls," Rob said as he glanced at his watch, "I'm expecting a call at five o'clock."

"From Stillwater?"

Rob nodded. "I think Regina may be able to come down for the dance Friday night. Her aunt and uncle live here, and she can stay with them."

"Rob, that's wonderful! I can't wait to meet her."

"I think you'll like her." He looked down at the floor, adding shyly, "I do."

Sara smiled fondly at her friend. She went over to the wastebasket and started rubbing the plaster off her hands, wishing Brad would talk that way about her. After she got most of the plaster off, she scrubbed her hands under the warm water in the sink. She thought about Caitlin and became angry all over again.

"And another thing," she said, turning off the faucet knobs forcefully, "Caitlin gets away with murder. It was enough to dress up the Brisco Indian as a member of the Cavalry team. But now Caitlin's going too far. Last night she gathered all the For Sale signs in Brisco and stuck them on the Brisco High School lawn."

"Oh, no," Rob said. "Sooner or later, Brisco is going to retaliate."

Sara grabbed a towel to dry her hands. "That's what I keep telling Janie, but she just laughs and says it's all in fun."

Rob scratched his head again. "I guess it is." He chuckled. "Just as long as things don't get out of hand."

Sara turned back to face the sink, secretly chiding herself for sounding so prudish. Her feelings were all jumbled up. It was ridiculous to get so upset over a few harmless pranks.

Rob bustled around the art room, trying to clean up and checking his watch a dozen times.

"Listen, Sara, I'd better run. I'll meet you here tomorrow. General Sheridan should be dry by then, and we can start to paint him."

Sara nodded. "And then on Friday we can assemble the whole thing, and then we'll be done."

Rob ran for the door, then turned and smiled. "Chin up!"

Sara listened to him race down the tiled hall. He was shouting, "A horse! A horse! My kingdom for a horse!"

At eleven o'clock on Friday morning a procession, led by Rob and Brad, carried the statue of General Sheridan onto the football field and placed him on his horse. It was the culmination of three weeks of hard work.

The float stood ready under the white goalposts. Six beautifully painted cardboard cutouts shone in the morning light. Surrounding the flatbed in bright blue and gold was a banner reading "THE CAVALRY. YESTERDAY'S HEROES—TODAY'S HOPE FOR THE FUTURE!"

The horse, which they had named Silver, stood at the head of the float with one hoof raised. It wasn't quite the sleek stallion that Rob had originally sketched—the Kleenex gave it a round, fluffy look. In fact, it looked more like a very large sheep dog extending its paw than a horse. But the real saddle and leather bridle did help a little.

"Hi! Ho! Silver, away!" Rob yelled triumphantly.

As if he were answering the call, General Sheridan slowly did a nose dive forward. His face ended up buried in the the horse's neck, and his hand looked like it was patting its nose.

"Whoa, big fella!" one of the guys yelled, and that set off a whole series of Lone Ranger jokes. Finally they found some wire and managed to secure General Sheridan in an upright position. The American flag was placed in his raised hand, and everyone shouted, "Charge!"

They were all in high spirits. The float was almost finished, and the big dance was that night.

Sara, in her paint-stained lab coat, was balanced on a milk crate putting the final touches on the general's beard. She dipped her brush in the can of brown paint she was holding, stood on tiptoe, and reached up.

"Wow, he looks fantastic!" Brad said, coming up behind her.

His voice startled her, and Sara jerked around to see who it was, losing her balance in the process. She stumbled off the milk crate and landed right in Brad's arms.

Sara's right arm was outstretched, still gripping the paint can. Her left had fallen over Brad's shoulder. They looked as if they were dancing.

Brad shook his head and laughed. "We seem to be on some kind of collision course!"

Sara giggled. "This must be what they mean when they say 'falling for each other.' " A look of surprise covered both their faces, and they quickly righted themselves. Sara couldn't believe she had said that!

She looked down at herself to make sure she hadn't spilled any paint and then lifted her head to look at Brad again. His brown eyes were studying her face, and he slowly bent toward her.

For one fleeting moment Sara thought he was going to kiss her, right there in front of everyone. Every muscle in her body tensed, waiting for it to happen.

She watched as his expression turned impish. "I thought only General Sheridan was supposed to have a beard," he said. He reached up with one hand and wiped the brown paint off her chin. "That's carrying your dedication a little too far."

Sara was feeling giddy, and before she knew it, she reached up and painted a moustache under Brad's nose.

That shocked him, and he leaped back. "Hey, what are you doing?"

"Serves you right," Sara said with a wicked smile. She dipped her brush into her paint can and walked menacingly toward him. "Now for the beard!"

Brad backed up and bumped the edge of the flatbed. "Truce!" he shouted, realizing it was a losing battle.

Sara laughed and hopped back onto the milk crate. "That'll teach you to tease an armed opponent." She dipped her brush into her can again and added, "This brush is loaded and could go off at any time."

Brad put his hands on his hips and smiled up at her. "Boy, put a brush in your hand and you turn into a whole different person."

Sara beamed back at him, thinking, *I do feel different. Janie and Rob would be proud of me.* Then, on impulse, she handed him her paint can and gestured for him to stand next to her.

As she painted, she could feel him studying her.

He watched in respectful silence and finally spoke in a halting voice. "Uh, Sara, I know it's kind of late to ask, but would you like to go to the dance with me tonight?"

Sara couldn't believe what she had just

heard. She spun around to face him, nearly falling off the crate again. He placed his hand on her waist to steady her. At his touch, she almost screamed, *Yes!*

He dropped his arm quickly and stared at the ground. Sara suddenly realized that he was embarrassed. It calmed her down a little, and she managed to say in a steady voice, "Sure, I'd love to."

He raised his head, and a look of relief shot across his face. "Great! I'll pick you up at seven-thirty." He started to walk away and then remembered he still had her paint can. Sheepishly, he handed it back to her.

Sara took the can and smiled warmly. He stood there looking at her, then tilted his head. "On second thought, make it six-thirty. We can to go out to dinner, too."

"Only if you have the moustache," Sara shot back, grinning. She laughed as his hand flew to his face. He'd forgotten all about it.

Brad recovered quickly. "Fine, but I absolutely refuse to be seen with a bearded lady!" He turned and leaped off the flatbed.

"Brad, wait!" Sara called. "You don't know where I live."

He cupped his hands around his mouth and yelled, "Yes, I do. Janie gave me your address."

A confused look crossed Sara's face. Janie hadn't mentioned talking to Brad.

"Remember," Brad called, pointing to his watch, "six-thirty!"

Sara's face lit up. She nearly exploded with happiness. She felt like dancing and singing at the top of her lungs. She wanted to hug her grandmother and her aunt Dorsie and Janie and Rob. Instead, she flung out her arms, let out a squeal of delight, and hugged the horse.

Chapter Nine

"You two look so pretty," their grandmother cooed.

Sara and Janie paraded across the living room and posed, trying to look as sophisticated as possible. They had tried on a hundred different outfits in the past two hours.

"I'd hate to see your room," Janie's mother said. "I'll bet it looks like a war zone."

Janie and Sara looked at each other and burst out laughing. It was true—the beds were covered with clothes and shoes, and every dresser drawer was wide open.

"It's hard to find the perfect outfit for the perfect date," Janie protested. "It's taken me three days to decide on this one."

She was wearing a clinging lavender knit dress that showed off her curves. She also wore white lace stockings and pumps and white crescent-shaped earrings. Janie pirouetted in a circle and grinned over her shoulder. Her dress was cut down in a low V in the back.

"I don't know about that back," her grandmother said with a frown. "Isn't it a little racy?"

"Well, at least it's the back and not the front," her daughter said.

Sara anxiously patted her dress. "I'm still not sure if mine was the right choice."

She had finally settled on a crisp white sleeveless dress with a scoop neck. It had a fitted bodice that flared into a full skirt. The dress showed off Sara's slim shoulders, and the royal blue belt she was wearing accentuated her small waist. Her hair hung in dark, shiny waves to her shoulders. For good luck she'd put on the string of pearls her parents had given her for her sixteenth birthday.

"You look so elegant," her grandmother said with a smile. "The spitting image of your mother."

That was the best compliment Sara could have received. She had always been envious of her mother's tall, easy grace and had always felt like an awkward colt next to her.

"Thanks, Gran," she said, feeling a little

misty eyed. "I wish Mom were here. That would make everything perfect."

"Oh, my gosh!" her aunt exclaimed, leaping from the couch and heading for the phone. "I almost forgot all about it."

"What?" they all said in unison.

"Your mom and dad called this afternoon, and they left a message." She anxiously shuffled through the drawer of the table. "Now where is it? I'm sure I wrote it down."

"I swear, Doris Keating, if your head weren't screwed on, you'd lose it!" Gran bustled over to her and joined in the search.

Sara's aunt slipped her glasses on her nose and peered behind the table. She grabbed an envelope and yelled, "Here it is!"

Sara stepped forward anxiously to receive the message, but her aunt recited it out loud. "Bill and Kitty will be here two weeks from today for a short visit."

Gran was appalled. "How in the world could you forget something as important as that?"

They started to bicker. Sara squealed and wrapped her arms around them. "Mom and Dad are coming!" she shouted.

A horn sounded out front, and Janie called, "They're here!" Everyone froze.

"Which one? Yours or mine?" Sara whispered.

Janie tiptoed to the picture window and peeked out. "Ours."

They all listened as the car doors slammed. They heard two male voices, then footsteps echoing on the wooden porch.

Suddenly the room was a whirl of activity. Janie and Sara's Gran ran to her bedroom, and Janie flew past Sara shouting, "I've got to check my makeup! Answer the door, Mom!"

Sara spun in a circle, trying to remember where she'd put her purse.

Her grandmother raced from the bedroom, waving a bottle. "This is my special 'knock 'em dead' perfume," she called. "Here, put some on."

Before Sara could protest, her grandmother had squirted Gardenia Mist all over her. Sara waved her hands frantically in front of her, trying to escape the overwhelming fragrance.

The doorbell rang, and Mrs. Keating paused to wince at her reflection in the hall mirror before pulling the door open. "Well, look who's here!" she said. "Come on in!"

Brad stepped through the door, and Sara nearly gasped out loud. He looked so handsome! He was wearing pleated tan linen pants, a yellow shirt, and an emerald green jacket.

Judd came in the door behind him, all spruced up but still wearing his familiar cowboy boots. Sara introduced them to her grandmother and aunt.

Her aunt placed her glasses on her nose and peered into Brad's face. "My, you're tall," she said with a giggle.

Sara's grandmother fluttered close by. "Don't you boys look nice."

The sound of Janie's feet thundering up the stairs made them all turn expectantly toward the kitchen.

She entered the living room slightly out of breath. "Oh, hi, you guys," she said casually. "I didn't know you were here."

The women all exchanged amused glances while Brad and Judd looked uncomfortable, anxious to leave.

"So, where are you all going for dinner?" Mrs. Keating finally asked.

"I thought we'd go to Parlato's for pizza," Judd said.

"That sounds wonderful!" Janie agreed.

Her mother and grandmother nodded their approval and then turned to beam at Brad.

He stuck his hands in his pockets. "I've

made reservations for two at a—uh—little out-of-the-way place."

The older women exchanged meaningful looks. "It sounds very romantic," they said almost together. They were winking and giggling and being anything but subtle.

Sara and Janie looked at each other, totally embarrassed. Then Janie grasped Judd's elbow and almost dragged him out the front door.

Janie's mother followed them all out onto the front porch. "You kids have a good time," she called. "And, Janie Keating, you fasten your seat belt!"

Janie stuck out her tongue at her mother and hopped into Judd's Jeep.

"Aren't they sweet!" Gran cooed, having trailed Sara and Brad out on the porch.

When Sara and Brad reached his car, her aunt yelled a final, "Don't stay out too late!"

Sara nodded and waved goodbye. Then she mumbled out of the corner of her mouth, "Sorry, Brad."

Brad held the car door open for her. "I don't mind. They're cute," he said. He shut the door and leaned in the open window, adding, "And so are you!"

* * *

Sara watched Brad drive with his hands resting easily on the steering wheel, and she smiled to herself. She realized that it was the first date she had ever had with a boy who drove a car. No wonder it felt so strange!

Brad must have sensed that she was watching him because he turned his head to look at her. "Not much longer now!" he said, flicking on the radio. His tanned hand drummed on the dashboard in time to the music, and Sara found herself humming along.

She leaned back in her seat and watched the houses fly by. A warm summer wind ruffled her hair, sending a shiver of excitement through her.

"Here's the last turn," Brad announced. "Hold on to your seat, it's a little bumpy."

They left the main highway and bounced down a gravel road. Sara leaned forward and scanned the countryside. *What can possibly be out here?* she wondered. It looked absolutely deserted. There wasn't a building or another car in sight.

"This certainly is 'out-of-the-way,' " Sara joked.

Brad gave her a mysterious smile. "It is, isn't it?"

A knot quickly formed in Sara's stomach. Was this what an actual date in a car meant?

Going to some deserted spot where she would be helpless? She shot him a concerned glance. He didn't look dangerous. But her hands gripped the dashboard as they drove slowly down the road.

They finally pulled onto the grass, and Brad stopped the car near a little grove of trees. He switched off the engine, set the emergency brake, and turned to face her.

Sara swallowed hard, thinking, *Oh, no, here it comes.* But nothing happened.

Brad's eyes danced with mischief as he watched her bewildered face. Then with a broad grin he announced grandly, "Madame, the coach has arrived." He reached in the backseat and lifted up a wicker picnic basket. "Dinner is served!"

Relief and surprise rushed through Sara, and she exploded into giggles. Brad, tickled with himself, leaped out of the car, then formally walked around to her door. She watched him toss a tablecloth over his arm with a flourish and swing open the door.

"Table for two?" he asked, bowing low. "Right this way."

Sara fought to control her giggles and put on her best British accent. "Thank you, kind sir. We'd like a table near the orchestra, preferably with a view."

Brad tried valiantly to keep a straight face as he offered her his arm. Sara giggled once more, then recovered and delicately linked her arm in his.

Together they followed a winding path through the trees up a hill. Sara's blue pumps kept sinking in the soft ground, causing her to stumble a few times. But she didn't mind at all.

"Close your eyes and don't open them until I tell you," Brad instructed, just before they reached the clearing at the top.

Sara squeezed her eyes shut and let Brad guide her the rest of the way. At the top Brad whispered, "OK. Now!"

Sara opened her eyes and marveled. She let go of Brad's arm and slowly stared at the scene before her. The land swept down from where they stood in a vast arc that ran unbroken to the horizon. The grandeur of the prairie overwhelmed her. The early-evening light covered everything in a warm lavender glow. Shimmering fields rippled in the wind like murmuring waves, and gigantic white clouds billowed above them, reaching up into the sky for miles. Shadows from the clouds raced along the ground and made the earth seem to shift and move as though it were alive and breathing. It was magnificent.

Brad quietly set the basket down and stood back. His eyes searched her face for her reaction. "I'm sure you've seen more spectacular views in your travels, but this is the best Fort Reno has to offer," he said shyly.

They stood in awed silence, gazing out over the prairie.

Finally Sara spoke. "You know, I've been lucky enough to see a lot of the world," she said quietly. "But I've never really gotten a chance to know the beauty of this country." She turned to face him, her eyes glistening. "Until now."

Brad thrust his hands in the pockets of his jacket. "This is my special spot," he confided. "I come here when life gets so complicated that I can't think straight anymore. I just stand here for a while and things don't seem so bad." He laughed self-consciously. "I guess that's pretty silly, isn't it."

Sara ran a hand through her hair. "No, it's not! I wish I'd known about this place sooner." She sighed. "I could have used it."

Brad shot her a questioning look. "You seem to be getting along fine here. You did a terrific job on the float."

Sara smiled up at him and then dropped her gaze to the ground. "Oh, the float's been fun, and Rob's been really nice. It's just that"

—she looked at the valley again—"sometimes I think that just because I've lived in other countries, people think I'm from another planet."

"They're just jealous," Brad reassured her. "Me included. I'd give anything to see the world." Then he added with a twinkle, "I'd give anything to see Missouri!"

He stood there with the wind ruffling his hair, and Sara couldn't help smiling. She shrugged her shoulders and said, "I guess it's just hard to be the new kid, no matter where you go."

Brad leaned slightly forward and looked into her downcast eyes. "You know, Sara, if you give us half a chance, we Okies aren't so bad."

His warm brown eyes met hers. He was open and understanding, and all she wanted to do was race into his arms and hide herself from the world. Brad took his hands from his pockets and moved a step toward her.

It felt as if a magnet were slowly pulling them together. She started to reach out, but the old look-before-you-leap part of her interfered. Instead of folding into his arms, she pulled back. "I'll help you with the tablecloth. This is a perfect spot for a picnic," she said in a shaky voice.

Brad stepped back, a little embarrassed about what had almost happened. He reached for the red-and-white checkered tablecloth. "Uh, sure," he stammered. "The orchestra seems to have taken a break." He handed her an edge of the cloth, and their hands touched. Brad gave her a mischievous smile. "But for just a moment, I thought I heard violins."

The dinner passed in a whirl of easy conversation. Sara was amazed at how comfortable she felt with Brad. Not once did she worry about spilling potato salad on her dress or saying the wrong thing.

Brad told her about growing up in Fort Reno with his three younger brothers. "Being the oldest has its good points and its bad points," he said, setting his paper cup on the picnic basket. "I get a lot of privileges my brothers don't get. But then, my parents expect me to set a good example for Chris, David, and Willy. Sometimes those guys can really be a pain. They ask a hundred questions about what I'm doing, and they always want to know where I'm going and why they can't come along." Brad chuckled. "I call them my watchdogs."

Sara laughed, trying to picture his brothers. She wondered if they were miniature versions of him.

"Going out to a restaurant is a major event in our house," Brad continued. "David and Willy always seem to start wrestling or hitting each other the minute they get to the table. They can never make up their minds about what to order, and something always gets spilled. I think waiters see the Ahyres family and turn and run the other way."

"I used to lie in bed at night pretending that I had brothers and sisters," Sara confided. "I had it all worked out. We'd live in a big, two-story house with a yard, swings, and a white picket fence. My dad would work at a bank, and my mom would stay home with us kids." She shrugged. "But so far, it hasn't worked out that way. They both love their jobs and have no intention of settling down anytime soon."

Brad poured some more cider in Sara's cup and asked, "What exactly do they do?"

"They're agronomists," Sara replied, taking a sip of her drink.

"What?" Brad asked, surprised. "I figured they must be with the CIA or something like that."

Sara laughed. "No, it's nothing as exotic as that. Basically they work in the science of crop production. They help underdeveloped countries manage their farmlands." She smoothed out her skirt. "That's why I'm here. They couldn't take me on this assignment."

"Where's that?"

Sara rolled her eyes, trying to keep a straight face. "Timbuktu."

Brad was reaching for his drink and nearly knocked it over. "Are you serious? You mean there really is such a place?"

"There really is. It's in Mali," Sara replied. "I know how you feel. I can't believe it, either."

Brad leaned back and kept shaking his head saying, "Wow!" Finally he gave her an impish grin. "So when you write your parents a letter, it goes from here—"

"To Timbuktu!" Sara chimed in with him. Brad threw his head back and laughed.

"That reminds me," she said, turning to Brad excitedly. "They're coming here to visit in a couple of weeks."

Brad clapped his hands together. "Sara, that's great!"

"I can't wait to see them," Sara said breathlessly. "They're so wonderful. My mom's from Oklahoma, and she and my dad met at Oklahoma State University in Stillwater. I think you'd like them, and I know they'd like you. You can meet them when they're here."

Sara suddenly stopped herself. It was only their first date, and she was already acting as though they were going steady. She gave Brad a sheepish look.

"I'd like to meet them," he said sincerely.

Sara blushed and began gathering the cups and plates to put back in the basket. *I like him*, she thought. *I mean, I really like him. It must be written all over my face.*

Brad knelt on one knee and opened the lid of the basket. "You know what my big dream is?" he asked, looking up at Sara. She shook her head. "It's to work really hard during the next year, save as much money as I can, and go to Europe after graduation. Then I'll come back and go to college."

Sara nodded enthusiastically. "That's great! I've always wanted to travel and sketch. You know, you can do it pretty cheaply if you stay in youth hostels. My friend Ilona and I bicycled through France last spring vacation and stayed in hostels the whole way. It cost us next to nothing."

"Maybe you could be my tour guide. You know, show me the ropes," he said casually as he dropped the silverware into the basket.

Sara beamed up at him. "That would be fun!" A voice inside her screamed, *Are you kidding? That would be heaven!*

Her deep blue eyes danced with excitement.

She began chattering about what he should plan to take and the best time of year to go. She was so excited that she folded the tablecloth herself and closed the lid of the basket before she noticed that Brad was standing and grinning at her.

A confused look crossed her face. "What's so funny?"

He reached out a hand to help her up and said with a playful glint in his eye, "You are! I've never seen you so excited before."

"I guess I got carried away," Sara said, blushing.

"You are incredibly cute," Brad said, holding her hand and studying her face. Then he did something that surprised both of them. He bent down and very carefully kissed her on the tip of her nose. They burst out laughing together.

"I'll race you to the car!" he called over his shoulder as he swooped up the picnic basket and charged down the hill.

Sara, giggling and running, shouted, "That's not fair! You had a head start!" She wanted that night to never end.

Chapter Ten

The dance was in full swing when Brad and Sara pulled into the parking lot. They could hear the music as they threaded their way between the cars, moving toward the gym. The beat was infectious, and they walked quickly.

At the door, Caroline was seated next to a card table taking tickets. She had pulled her dark hair into a ponytail and tied it with a huge fuchsia net bow. She was nodding her head in time to the music.

Caroline looked up from her cashbox, and her eyes widened with surprise. "Sara," she shouted over the music, "you look wonderful!"

Sara was bubbling inside. She wanted to hug the whole world. "So do you!" she shouted back, flashing a big smile. "I love your dress!"

Caroline stamped their hands with a rubber stamp as the band began a Bruce Springsteen song. A shout went up from the crowd, and Brad yelled, "All right, the Boss!"

His whole body was bouncing with the beat as he leaned over to Sara. "Come on, let's catch this song. It's one of my favorites!" His lips brushed her ear, sending a tingle through her entire body. He grabbed Sara's hand and practically skipped toward the center of the gym. They squeezed between two other couples and started dancing.

The song connected everyone on the floor, and Sara found herself shouting the words to the song and clapping along with Brad.

When the song ended, everyone applauded and gathered in little groups waiting for the music to start again. Sara looked around the gym. The basketball hoops had been raised and multicolored kites were hanging everywhere. Many were made out of Mylar and twinkled in the light. The theme was "Flying High," and Sara was soaring with happiness.

"Sara!" She heard someone call her name and scanned the crowd to see who it was. Across the floor, she could see a curly-topped head bouncing up and down and a pair of arms waving. Janie was bellowing in her best cheerleading voice. Sara's hand shot up into the air, and she started to holler back. But just then, the band struck up an old Beatles song, and everyone stampeded back onto the floor.

Brad spun her around and started dancing. He was really a good dancer, and it was easy to follow his lead. She could feel people watching them, and for the first time she wasn't self-conscious. They were perfect together. She tossed her head with a flair, her long, shiny hair catching the light. In one move, he twirled her toward him and then spun her out again.

Her arm flew out and struck someone. Sara turned to mouth an apology. Caitlin turned at the same time to see who had hit her. Her smile hardened when she recognized Sara. For a split second Sara's whole body tensed. But Brad swung her back into his arms, and they disappeared into the crowd.

"I'm dying of thirst," Brad finally gasped. Their faces were rosy from the exertion. "Let's go get a soda."

Sara nodded vigorously, still trying to catch her breath. He placed his hand on the small of her back and gently guided her through the crowd to the refreshment stand.

"Wait here. I'll be right back." Sara watched him thread his way toward the stand, stopping to say "hi" and chat with people. *Every-body likes him*, she thought proudly as a tiny smile crossed her face, *and he's with me!*

Her thoughts were interrupted by a voice calling her name. "Sara. So, I see you got a date after all."

She turned to see Caitlin smiling sweetly at her. She looked picture perfect. The soft pink of her dress gave her complexion a special glow, and her hair was drawn up on the sides in pearl and pink combs, showing off her high cheekbones and pert nose. *She looks terrific, and she knows it*, Sara thought angrily.

"Yeah," Sara said, smiling back at Caitlin. "I guess I got lucky." She wasn't going to let anyone spoil her evening.

Fortunately, Lizzie, one of the cheerleaders, and Suzanna rushed up right then. They said hello to Sara and then turned their attention to Caitlin.

"You look absolutely gorgeous!" Suzanna gushed.

"Where's your date?" Lizzie asked, spinning in a circle. "I hear he's from OSU."

Suzanna nodded. "Yeah, we're all dying to meet him!"

Caitlin turned her head and put on a beaming smile. "Josh insisted on getting me something to drink. He's over there. You can't miss him." Sara watched her make a sweeping gesture toward the refreshment stand. "He's the one with the frat pin."

Sara searched the crowd to see whom she could be talking about. Her gaze settled on a short, plump guy with glasses and dark hair. That couldn't be the fabulous date Caitlin had been talking about! She glanced back at Caitlin and watched her nervously glancing over her shoulder in his direction. Caitlin definitely looked embarrassed. It suddenly occurred to Sara that Caitlin had probably never met the guy before that night.

At that moment Brad arrived with their drinks. Sara took a big gulp and smiled when she saw Janie bouncing toward her.

"You guys looked like Fred Astaire and Ginger Rogers out there!" Janie said.

"More like Fred and Ethel Mertz!" Sara said with a laugh. She watched Brad turn to talk with some friends and whispered to Janie, "He's the dancer, not me. I don't know my left from my right."

Janie squeezed her arm encouragingly and ran off in search of Judd.

"My, my, Miss Sara. You certainly look lovely tonight!"

Sara turned to see Rob grinning at her over a polka-dot bow tie. She fluttered her eyelids at him. "Why, thank you, Mr. Proctor. That certainly is an unusual cravat you're wearing this evening."

Rob waved his hand like a fan. "Only the best for the Sooner Dance," he drawled. "I caught your act on the dance floor," he whispered confidentially. "You and Brad seem to be doing just fine."

Sara giggled and whispered back, "Where's Regina?"

Rob shook his head. "She couldn't make it tonight."

"Oh, Rob," Sara said sympathetically, "I'm so sorry."

He held up his hand. "All is not lost. She's going to try to come tomorrow for the parade."

Sara smiled at him. "I really hope she can make it." She was holding her hair up off her neck with one hand and balancing her drink with the other. The crowd seemed to abruptly shift, jostling her forward. She let go of her hair and reached out toward Rob to catch her balance.

Someone bumped her, and she heard Rob shout, "Look out!"

The cold soda made her leap back, but it was too late. She stared down in horror at the huge stain on the front of her white dress. Rob took the cup from her hand and was trying to brush the remaining drips onto the floor.

"Gosh, I'm so clumsy," Sara stammered.

"It's not your fault," said a familiar voice. "There are just too many people over here." Sara looked up to see Caitlin and started wiping her dress and gesturing helplessly toward the ice and Coke on the floor.

Caitlin took charge. "Rob, see if you can get some paper towels to clean up the floor. I'll take Sara to the bathroom." She hooked her arm in Sara's. "With a little cold water, that stain will come right out," she reassured Sara.

"I don't know how it happened," Sara said, looking confused. "I should have been more careful."

Before Sara knew what was happening, Caitlin was ushering her toward the bathroom. She paused long enough to tell Brad, who had missed the whole event, "I'm not stealing your date. We just have a little problem to solve."

Brad turned and saw Sara trying to hold the sticky dress away from her body. His brow furrowed with concern, but Sara shrugged her shoulders and giggled sheepishly as they hurried off through the crowd.

In the bathroom Sara wiped furiously at the stain. "Oh, Brad must think I'm a total klutz!" Her embarrassment had turned to anger at herself. She ran another paper towel under the cold water and attacked her dress again.

"Calm down," Caitlin said. "It's no big deal. These things happen to the best of us." She moved Sara toward the sink and held her hem under the running water. "Oh, it's coming out just fine."

Sara leaned forward to let the water run down the top of her dress. The stain was coming out, but she was getting soaked in the process.

When she was finished, Sara stood back and faced the mirror. Her shoulders slumped miserably. "I can't go back out there like this! I look like I've been through a hurricane!"

Caitlin put her arm around Sara and smiled at her in the mirror. "Don't worry. It'll dry in no time. Besides, there are so many people out there, who'll notice?"

"Brad will!" Sara wailed. She turned and punched the button on the hand dryer and held her skirt under the hot air.

Caitlin reached into her tiny leather purse and pulled out some lipstick. "Oh, don't worry about Brad. He won't care. He's too nice a guy."

Sara's face softened as she thought of Brad. She smiled warmly. "He is, isn't he."

Caitlin nodded. "Everyone turns to him for advice and help." She leaned forward to study her reflection while keeping an eye on Sara. "I'm sure that's why Janie felt she could call him."

Sara knitted her brow and watched Caitlin slowly trace the outline of her lips. "Of course," Caitlin added, "he is the student council president, so he had to be here anyway. But Janie needed help, and he came right to her rescue."

Sara let go of her dress and stepped away from the dryer. "What are you talking about?"

"Your date with Brad," Caitlin said innocently, putting the cap back on her lipstick. She reached for a paper towel to blot her lips. "When I turned Brad down, Janie knew he didn't have a date. Neither did you, so she asked him to do her a favor and take you."

"What?" Sara put her hand to her head and squinted at Caitlin. She couldn't believe what she was hearing.

Caitlin turned toward Sara dramatically,

her eyes open wide. "You knew about that, didn't you?"

Sara stood there, stunned. She hadn't known. She had had no idea. But she wasn't about to embarrass herself further in front of Caitlin. Sara looked her square in the eye. "Oh, that. Yes. We worked it all out together."

Sara reached calmly into her shoulder bag, pulled out her brush, and yanked it through her hair with quick brisk strokes, trying to think.

Caitlin gave a loud sigh of relief. "I didn't think Janie would do something like that without telling you about it. She's too sweet."

Sara gathered all her strength and smiled at Caitlin in the mirror. "Yes, she's great."

Brad's words at the float suddenly rang in her ears. He had said that he'd gotten her address from Janie. Sara could feel her throat tighten, and she knew if she stayed in there another minute, she would start crying.

Somehow she managed to put her brush back in her purse and thank Caitlin for her help. Her eyes welled with tears as she pulled the door open to leave. She had to find Janie!

Chapter Eleven

"All right, I called him," Janie confessed when Sara found her. "But I was only trying to help!"

"How could you? I have never been so embarrassed in my whole life! Brad must think I'm a total jerk."

"He does not." Janie reached out to touch Sara's arm. "He likes you. Look how much fun you were having dancing. I never would have called him if I didn't think—"

Sara angrily shook her hand away. "Oh, sure! He was just being nice, that's all."

Thinking back to how she had danced so flirtatiously with him and all the things she had said at their picnic, Sara buried her face in her hands.

She and Janie were standing just outside

the gym door on the sidewalk. Janie glanced anxiously in at the dance and then moved Sara farther from the door to console her. "Look, he wouldn't have asked you if he didn't want to go with you."

Sara flung her head up. "Caitlin said Brad was doing you a *big* favor. And by the way," she added, crossing her arms angrily in front of her, "how did Caitlin know about it? Or did you all get together and decide to help 'poor' Sara out?"

Janie reached for her arm again. "No!"

"How many other people know about this?" Sara practically yelled.

"Caitlin's the only one," Janie assured her. "I swear."

Sara put her hands on her hips. "What's to stop her from telling everyone else?"

That idea hadn't occurred to Janie. She nervously kicked the brick wall and said defensively, "I couldn't help it. She made me tell her."

"Made you?" Sara said sarcastically. "What did she do, threaten to beat you up?"

"No, it's just that she was really upset about you and Brad and well . . ." Janie threw her arms in the air and sighed. "You don't understand. She's the captain of the cheerleading squad, and I didn't want her to hate me and—"

She shook her head. "You just don't under-stand."

Sara shook her head sadly. "I guess I don't. And I don't think I want to." Her chin was starting to quiver again, and her face twisted into an ugly frown. "I'm sure you've all had a lot of fun laughing at me. You and your stupid hick friends."

Janie looked like she'd been slapped. "Now wait a minute. That's not true!"

Sara lurched backward. "Well, my parents will be here soon, and I'm going to leave with them, so you can keep your silly dances and your idiotic cheerleading!" Sara turned and started to run. "I don't care if I ever see you again!"

As she ran she heard Janie shout in a choked voice, "Go ahead and run, see if I care!"

Sara stumbled blindly through the parking lot as painful images flashed through her mind: Caitlin, smiling smugly at her in the mirror, knowing everything; the picnic on the hill—Brad hadn't even wanted to be seen with her at a restaurant; her grandmother and Janie's condescending smiles at the dinner table the night before. Everyone had conspired to make fun of her!

"Sara, wait up!" She heard Brad pounding behind her. "What's the matter?"

Sara bolted from the parking lot and raced as hard as she could toward the football field. Her side ached. "Leave me alone!" she screamed back at him.

Ahead, she could see the goalposts outlined in the moonlight. Directly under them was the float. She clutched her side and limped toward it.

"Sara, stop!" Brad called. He caught her arm, and she turned to give him an angry look.

"Why did you run out of the dan—" He stopped in midsentence. A look of horror crossed his face as he stared over her shoulder. Sara turned quickly to see what had caused it.

The float. Where was it? Headlights from the parking lot flashed past and for one eerie moment, the space where it had been was lit up. But everything was different! Brad let go of Sara's arm and raced toward the float.

He and Sara stopped a little distance away. She couldn't believe what she saw.

All the cutouts of the students were gone as was General Sheridan. In his place on the horse there was a cardboard cutout of the Brisco High Indian. The skirt of the float was missing, and a new banner had been draped over the Indian that read, "The Joke's On You." But worst of all—the flatbed was missing. They would have no float.

"I knew something like this would happen if they kept up their pranks," Brad muttered, pulling angrily at the banner.

Sara shook her head in despair. Her eyes filled with fresh tears as she thought of all the hours of hard work they had put in on it.

Someone touched Sara on the shoulder, and she looked up at Rob. "What are you doing here?" she asked, trying to hold back the tears.

"I discovered this mess half an hour ago. I've been trying to figure out how to fix it since then." He walked toward the remains of the float with his hands shoved in his pockets and his shoulders hunched. "I would have told y'all about it, but I didn't want to spoil your fun."

Brad shot a glance at Sara, and they both looked away quickly. Brad turned his back to them and kicked halfheartedly at the horse.

Rob, sensing the tension between them, gave Sara a questioning look. She met his gaze and shook her head brusquely.

"It looks like the cavalry has lost this battle," Brad said dejectedly.

The three of them stood there in a miserable silence. Finally, in an effort to cheer them up, Rob lifted the banner and draped it around his shoulders. "We could all march in the parade wearing the banner and carrying the horse," he suggested. "That would show Brisco that you can't keep the better school down."

Sara started giggling. She started to make little hiccupping noises, which made Brad and Rob laugh. Rob tossed a corner of the banner at Sara, and she covered her head with a loud snort.

Suddenly she let out a little cry and raised the banner. Her eyes were wide with excitement.

"I've got an idea!" The serious tone of her voice caused Rob and Brad to stop laughing. "This may sound silly, but bear with me." They both stared at her expectantly.

Sara took a deep breath and began slowly. "Last February I was in Switzerland for *Fasching*. It's sort of like a German Mardi Gras. They celebrate it with costume parties, dances, and parades. Anyway, one parade in Basel included a lot of bands and this human float."

Rob and Brad looked puzzled, and Sara continued her explanation. "You see, these people covered themselves with this huge piece of material that they had painted. There must have been about fifty people under it. They marched along, moving it so that it looked as if the scene they had painted were alive!"

The two boys looked at each other in confusion. "So?" Rob asked.

"So," Sara said, placing the banner on her head to demonstrate. "We could do the same thing!"

"Where could we possibly get that much material by morning?" Brad asked.

Sara knit her brow and started pacing. "I don't know. If we can't find any, maybe we could use cardboard boxes of some kind instead. But we'd need big ones."

"How big?" Brad asked.

Sara stopped and looked at him. "Full body size. Big enough for a person to march inside of."

"Oh, I get it!" Brad said excitedly. "Then we could paint a scene on the outside, and that way we wouldn't need the flatbed. We'd be a human float!"

Sara nodded vigorously. She started pacing again. "But we'd need a lot of boxes so we could make a huge marching mural that could change as different sides of the boxes were out."

Rob snapped his fingers. "Refrigerator boxes!"

Brad turned. "What did you say?"

Rob looked up and shouted, "I said, refrigerator boxes!"

"Where could we get them at this time of the night?" Sara asked.

"Proctor Appliance and Electric!" Rob said.

Brad joined him, shouting, "His dad owns the store!"

They huddled together in a circle, excitedly looking at one another. "We'd need paint. And brushes," Sara said breathlessly.

"I could probably get Mr. Maier to open the art room," Brad added helpfully.

"Who's Mr. Maier?" Sara asked.

"The principal. He's already here chaperoning the dance."

"You know, this idea is so farfetched," Brad whispered, "that it just might work."

They all nodded eagerly.

"I'll get my dad to open the store and lend us as many boxes as he has."

"We could paint two scenes on the boxes and then switch them during the parade," Sara suggested.

Brad jumped in. "Just like a Rubik's Cube!"

"But we can't do this alone," Rob said. "Brad, you go tell Caroline to gather the forces."

Sara started to bite her nails. "I'll go home and get all of my supplies, and I'll draw the designs. We can keep the same idea that we had, but the first scene will be the past, and when we switch sides, it'll show the future."

"The theme has to be written somewhere on the float," Rob pointed out.

Sara looked at the banner lying on the ground and exclaimed, "Two kids could march in front of the float carrying a banner and our two flags."

Brad checked his watch. "We've only got about twelve hours until the parade at ten o'clock tomorrow. If we work all night, we just might be able to do it!" Then he grabbed Sara, who was still working it out in her head, and squeezed her tight. "Sara, you're a genius!"

Sara tensed, suddenly remembering what Caitlin had said. But then she abruptly put it out of her mind. They had a job to do!

Brad dropped his arms quickly and suddenly looked embarrassed.

"Sara," Rob said, stepping forward. "I'll give you a ride to your house." He looked over at Brad. "We'll all meet back here as quickly as possible. OK?"

Brad nodded and turned to run toward the gym. Sara and Rob started to race for the parking lot, when they heard Brad shout, "I have one last question."

"What?" Rob and Sara both asked.

"Is this whole thing as ridiculous as I think it is?"

Rob and Sara looked at each other, then back at Brad. "Yes!" they yelled back.

Brad waved. "Just wanted to make sure. See you both in about an hour."

Chapter Twelve

At eight forty-five the next morning, Sara paused for her first break since she had started painting the night before. She plopped her brush against the paint can and stood up shakily. Every part of her body seemed to creak. She squinted in the bright morning light. *When did the sun come up?* she wondered.

The artwork was nearly done, and Sara stepped back to survey the results. Twelve freshly painted cardboard boxes stood glistening in the sun. She shook her head. "It's a miracle!"

It was hard to believe that less than eleven hours earlier they had discovered the disaster.

Sara stretched her arms above her head, arching her back. Then she looked down at herself. Her dress was ruined. Paint and grass stains were everywhere, and it was wrinkled beyond recognition. But Sara didn't care.

During the night she had thrown on her lab coat and hastily tied her hair up in a ponytail. She rubbed her bloodshot eyes and headed for the makeshift refreshment table.

Her grandmother and her aunt and some other parents had answered their distress call with sandwiches, cookies, and thermoses filled with hot chocolate and coffee. Sara reached for the plaid thermos holding the coffee and poured herself a cup. She took a sip and let the past few hours run through her mind.

Word of the disaster had spread fast, and people came out of the woodwork to help. Mr. Maier, the principal, had been a lifesaver. He turned on the football field lights so they could work, donated his red pickup truck for hauling the boxes, and stayed up all night to help paint.

When the truck had arrived, Rob was kneeling in the back, clutching five refrigerator boxes. He looked defeated.

"My dad said this is all he had," he had said in a miserable voice.

That had been the first big setback of the evening. They needed at least twelve boxes for the human float to look right. But a number of the parents had searched for big boxes. Fortunately, Mrs. LeVan, one of Sara's grandmother's bridge partners, still had some wardrobe boxes from her recent move. They were almost the same height as the refrigerator boxes, and at a distance they would look the same.

About four in the morning the football lights had suddenly clicked off because they were on a timer. Mr. Maier had gone off on an errand, and nobody else knew how to turn them back on. They had been about to give up when a car engine started up and a pair of headlights shone onto the field.

The field was suddenly filled with the sound of running feet, car doors slamming, and engines roaring. For a few minutes it was like a demolition derby, with cars driving in all directions. Another set of headlights lit up the field. Then another, and another until the entire football field was ablaze with light.

"Hup, two, three, four!" Janie rasped from the far side of the field. Her voice was hoarse from shouting, but her energy hadn't flagged. Sara took another sip of coffee and laughed as she watched the weary marchers staggering around in formation, trying to obey Janie's orders.

The choreography had been more difficult than they had thought. Trying to get the right scenes to show at the same time was complicated. Luckily, Janie had volunteered to work it all out. Good old Janie had managed to talk Judd into joining the group. Caroline was also out there in her baseball cap, trying to keep her eyes open. Sara smiled fondly at Janie again. A look of guilt crossed Sara's face as she thought of the angry words she had said to Janie. She wanted to run over and apologize, but there wasn't enough time and it wasn't the right place. Sara shivered, thinking, *I'll deal with it later.*

Just then Janie yelled, "Parade rest!" Twelve people flopped onto the grass, exhausted.

Sara reached for a peanut-butter cookie, suddenly realizing that she was starving. Her picnic on the hill with Brad had been hours before. She devoured the cookie in two bites, grabbed another, and turned to watch some kids fill in the last of her designs.

It actually looks great, Sara thought as she took another sip of coffee. *I can't believe it!* Her gaze swept the whole group of people, and she shook her head again.

"What are you smiling at?" Brad asked, reaching for the thermos.

Sara turned, surprised to see him. He'd

been there all night, but they really hadn't talked since the initial planning stages. She had been busy painting, and he had been gathering supplies and running errands.

"I can't believe this town," she said, pushing some wisps of hair out of her face. "Everyone's been so supportive. They're just incredible."

Brad looked at her over the top of his cup of coffee. "I told you that if you give us half a chance, we Okies aren't so bad."

Sara met his steady gaze and opened her mouth to speak. She wanted to tell him she was sorry for acting like a jerk earlier. She had been thinking about it all night. Even if Janie had arranged their date, they had had fun together. At least until she had spilled her drink and seen Caitlin. She had been so upset at the time that it hadn't occurred to her that maybe it had been Caitlin who bumped her arm. And however it happened, Sara knew she had overreacted. She wanted to let Brad know that she cared.

"Everybody listen up!" Rob suddenly called from the back of Mr. Maier's truck. Brad set his cup down on the table and quickly moved over to listen.

Sara placed her cup beside his and heaved a sigh. She would just have to wait until later to talk to Brad. Wearily, she moved toward the gathering.

"Now, remember, don't get too close together," Rob instructed the marchers. "The paint's not quite dry and you could smear it. We've cut eyeholes in each box, and hopefully you'll be able to see where you're going."

"If you get lost just follow my voice," Janie tried to say. But only hoarse squeaking sounds came from her throat.

Rob grinned wickedly. "Yeah, just listen for old froggy here."

Brad hopped up onto the truck, and he and Rob talked to each other for a moment. Then Brad turned to face the group. "I have some good news and some bad news. The good news is—we're finished!" Cheers and whistles rose up from the crowd. "The bad news is"—he pointed to his watch—"we have to be at the top of Rock Island Road at nine-thirty, in about a half an hour."

A chorus of good-hearted boos answered him. One of the girls complained. "When are we going to get a chance to change our clothes?"

Brad raised his arms to quiet them, then spoke in an earnest voice. "You've all done a tremendous amount of work on an impossible job, and I—uh—I just want to say that you're the best group of people and friends that anybody could have."

Sara watched Brad's face fill with emotion, and she started to get misty eyed herself. He looked so vulnerable that she wanted to race up and throw her arms around him.

Brad continued, "Well, what are we waiting for? Let's get going!" He raised his fist, and everyone called in unison, "Charge!"

People ran in all directions, hoisting boxes onto trucks and jumping in cars. Last-minute instructions were shouted as everyone sprang into action.

Rob caught Sara's hand. "Come on. You ride with me. We can watch the parade when it hits Main Street and then follow it into Heritage Park." He followed her gaze and saw she was still looking at Brad, who was talking to Janie. "Along the way, maybe we can sort out your love life!" he added.

People had poured into Fort Reno for the big parade from all over Canadian County. Main Street had been thronged with hordes of onlookers, waving flags and cheering as each school band and float m. ched by. Sara and Rob had run alongside the marching boxes, shouting encouragement to the kids inside. Janie ran them through their paces perfectly, using a police whistle to get their attention over the noise of the spectators. She would punch Judd who'd shout out each command, and the crowd "ooh"-ed and "ah"-ed as the picture changed before their startled eyes.

After the parade was over, everybody jammed into Heritage Park to await the judges' decision. Sticky-fingered children held the strings of brightly colored balloons. The delicious aromas of popcorn and hot dogs rose up from booths manned by the Rotary Club and different church groups. The bandshell was draped with flags and striped bunting, and the Kiwanis Club band bravely attempted to play a version of "You're a Grand Old Flag."

Sara squinted in the noonday sun and stood on tiptoe, searching for Brad. She couldn't spot one familiar face in the milling crowd. Sara turned for a better look.

"Any sign of him?" Rob asked her.

She shook her head. "No such luck." She hadn't seen Brad anywhere along the parade route, and now in the park he was nowhere to be found.

"Sara! Over here!" Her aunt and grandmother were waving at them by the bandstand, balancing hot dogs and huge cups of lemonade. Sara and Rob threaded their way over, and she quickly introduced him.

Her aunt Dorsie waggled her mustard-covered hot dog at Rob. "Oh, you're the good friend of Sara's we've heard so much about."

Rob grinned crookedly and started to reply. But suddenly, every freckle on his face seemed to light up. Sara turned to see what had caused the sudden transformation. There, a short distance away, stood Regina. Sara recognized her from Rob's photograph, and she looked a little dazed and confused in all the bustle. Rob didn't take his eyes off her for a second. "Excuse me, I've got to go," he mumbled.

Regina spotted Rob at the same time, burst into a huge grin, and ran in his direction. Sara watched him scoop her up in his arms and spin her around. Rob was at least a foot taller than Regina, all elbows and ankles. She was short and round and freckle faced. Sara decided they were perfect for each other. Rob slipped Regina's hand into his, and they quickly disappeared into the crowd. Sara smiled at seeing her friend so happy.

Out of the corner of her eye, she watched one of the painted refrigerator boxes bump its way toward her. People backed out of its path, pointing and laughing hysterically. As the box drew closer, Sara could hear Janie clowning around inside. Sticking out of the bottom were four feet, and there seemed to be some kind of discussion going on inside, because she could hear voices giggling and laughing. The box kept lurching forward as elbows jabbed the sides and feet tripped over feet.

Finally the box lumbered clumsily to a halt. Sara watched in amazement as the two small red tennis shoes in the front turned to face the two large cowboy boots in the back.

Mrs. Keating, looking on amused, suddenly choked on her hot dog. "Those look like Janie's shoes!" she exclaimed.

"And Judd's boots!" Sara laughed.

Sara's aunt strode purposefully up to the box. She rapped her knuckles on the side. "Janie Keating! Are you in there?"

There was a screech, then Janie said in a muffled whisper, "It's my mother!" The two pairs of shoes tried to leap apart, nearly knocking the box over.

Two green eyes peered cautiously out of the eye holes, and a meek little voice answered, "Yes, Mother?"

"You come out of there this instant!" her mother ordered. She turned to the small crowd that had gathered and shrugged helplessly.

"She's my daughter, and I don't know what to do with her."

Meanwhile, the box started to tiptoe backward, out of sight. Sara saw it and quietly followed. She gently knocked on the side.

"Janie? It's me, Sara." The box stopped still. "Listen, I'm really sorry about all those awful things I said last night. I was just upset about everything. I didn't really mean them. Can we be friends again? I really think you're the greatest cousin a girl could ask for." Sara raised her head and watched two green eyes fill with tears.

"Oh, Sara!" Janie cried. She struggled to get out of the box, but just then it tumbled forward, knocking Sara over in the process.

As she fell back, Sara heard Judd yell, "Whoa, wait a minute!"

Then all three of them hit the ground with a thud. The absurdity of the situation seized Sara, and she doubled up with laughter. Janie and Judd wriggled the rest of the way out of the box and rolled on the grass, howling and clutching their sides.

"May I have your attention, please!" came a voice over the loudspeaker. "The judges have reached their decision, and we will be announcing the winners of the Sooner Days Parade very shortly."

Sara and Janie gasped and staggered to their feet. With their arms wrapped around each other, they skipped over to Gran and Aunt Dorsie, who hadn't even noticed they were gone. Rob appeared beside them, with Regina. Sara gave her a warm welcome and then scanned the crowd anxiously for Brad. There was still no sign of him.

An expectant hush came over the crowd as the mayor stepped out on the stage and walked to the microphone. He adjusted the stand, then tapped the microphone with his fingers.

"Is this thing on?" he asked of the faces looking up at him.

"Yes!" everyone shouted back good-naturedly.

"Well, then," the mayor said, smiling over his glasses. "Every year we are treated to a wonderful Sooner Days celebration from all the fine people of Canadian County. And this year is no exception." He scratched his head thoughtfully. "I want to take a moment here to thank the schools who entered this year's float competition. Let's give them all a big hand!"

When the applause died down, the mayor cleared his throat and continued. "Well, I guess you all want to know who the winners are," he said.

"Yes!" a thousand voices roared.

"OK, here goes! In the float competition, third prize goes to Silver City Senior High!"

There was a round of applause as the delegation from Silver City went up to the stage and accepted their ribbon.

"Second prize goes to Concho High School!"

There was another burst of cheering. Janie and Sara clutched each other, and they both held their breath.

"First prize goes to—" the mayor paused, then started again. "You know, we've had some great winners over the years, but this year is something special. I've never seen such originality and inventiveness in this competition. So, by unanimous decision of the judges, the blue ribbon goes to Fort Reno High!"

A whoop went through the crowd. Everyone hugged the nearest person. Janie squeezed Sara. Then she flung her arms around Judd's neck. Sara hugged Rob, who was hugging Regina.

Suddenly someone grabbed Sara's hand and began pulling her through the swirling mass of people. She couldn't see who it was, but she followed blindly. She looked back and saw Rob close behind her, grinning.

When they reached the stage, Sara realized who it was.

"Brad, I'm sorry—" she started to say. But he told her to be quiet, then tucked his arm through hers. Rob came up beside her on the other side, and they ushered her up the steps to the stage.

Brad stepped up to the microphone and held the blue ribbon over his head. "I'd like to accept this prize on behalf of all the students at Fort Reno High." A burst of cheering greeted his announcement.

He raised both hands to quiet the crowd. "But there's one special person that we should all thank." Sara turned and smiled at Rob, ready to applaud him. "Without her, we could never have done it." He stepped back and looked at Sara. "Sara Arandel!"

Sara's hands flew to her face, and she turned beet red. The applause was deafening. Behind her the band struck up the Oklahoma "fight" song, "Boomer Sooner."

The crowd started to clap in rhythm to the music. Rob jumped up to the microphone and led them in chanting, "Sara Sooner!"

Grateful tears welled up in her eyes as Sara looked out at the faces in the crowd. Her grandmother and aunt were waving madly, telling everyone around them she was their niece and granddaughter. Janie was jumping all over Judd, hollering in her best cheerleader voice, which had miraculously recovered.

A strange sensation came over Sara as she realized that she really belonged there. She wanted to stretch out her arms and hug every last smiling face. But there was one person she wanted to embrace more than anyone else in the world.

With a rush of warmth, she turned to look at Brad. But before she had a chance to do anything, her grandmother and aunt raced up the steps and smothered her in hugs and kisses. She finally untangled herself and looked around for Brad again.

He was gone! The mayor was still there, and Rob—but where was Brad? She shot Rob a bewildered look. He bent down and whispered in her ear. She looked up at him quizzically. He nodded, then pointed over her shoulder. She spun around, and a huge smile slowly spread across her face.

Chapter Thirteen

There, behind the bandshell, was Brad's car. Sara could see him behind the wheel, grinning. He motioned for her to join him. She gave Rob a grateful hug and flew down the steps.

Sara's heart was pounding in her chest. It was the moment she had been waiting for. She had rehearsed it in her mind all night. Brad jumped out of the car and held the door open for her. Sara's footsteps quickened. She knew exactly what she had to say.

From out of nowhere, Caitlin stepped in front of her. "Brad!" she purred. "You brought your car! Why don't we go celebrate!" She hadn't even noticed Sara standing behind her.

"We can stop at The Scoop," Caitlin suggested sweetly. "My treat!"

"Sorry, Caitlin," Brad said, never taking his eyes off Sara. "I've already got a date."

Caitlin followed his gaze to Sara. Her face fell in disappointment. "Oh. With Sara," she said, forcing a smile. Sara eyed her coolly.

Caitlin giggled shrilly. "I should have guessed," she said. She backed away, mumbling something about having to go find Peter Silbert. Sara and Brad weren't listening. They only had eyes for each other.

Sara slid across the car seat and turned to face Brad. Suddenly she felt a wave of panic. She didn't know how to begin. They looked at each other awkwardly.

"Look," they both said at the same time.

They paused, then said simultaneously, "What were you going to say?"

They both laughed, and Brad finally said, "OK, you go first."

"Well," Sara said, taking a deep breath, "I wanted to say that I'm sorry for running out of the dance." She bit her lip nervously. "Janie told me she'd asked you to take me, and I got upset, so I ran away." She looked down at her hands. "What I'm trying to say is that I'd like us to be friends, even though . . ." She shrugged. "You know."

Brad reached across the seat and lightly touched Sara's shoulder. "Janie forgot to tell you one important thing. My side of the conversation."

Sara looked up, her deep blue eyes studying his face.

Brad smiled sheepishly. "I wanted to ask you to the dance all along, but I thought you and Rob were going together and I didn't want to interfere."

"I thought you were with Caitlin!" Sara confessed.

He grinned and shook his head.

"What?" Sara asked, smiling at him.

Brad kept shaking his head, his eyes twinkling. "I can't get over how pretty you are."

His words surprised her, and Sara looked down, embarrassed.

"It's true. Ever since that day in the park, I've been trying to get up enough courage to ask you out." Sara felt him edge closer to her. "When you signed up for the float committee, I thought it was my lucky day."

Sara smiled and said shyly, "I'm pretty sure it was mine."

She tilted her head up to look at him. They sat there quietly, gazing into each other's eyes.

Brad cocked his head and slowly grinned. "Sara Sooner, did you ever hear of an 'Oklahoma Hello'?"

He slowly leaned toward her and gently brushed her lips with a kiss. It felt almost like a whisper.

Brad rumbled huskily, "Hello."

"Hello back," she answered dreamily.

Sara raised her hand to touch his hair. It was as soft as she had imagined it would be, and she smiled into his warm brown eyes. Sara wanted to memorize every feature of his face so that she'd never forget that moment.

"Sara," he said quietly, "you're terrific."

His arms wrapped around her and their lips met in a lingering kiss. She thought she would melt into the floor. Sara nestled her head on his shoulder and closed her eyes. She could have stayed there forever.

Suddenly Brad tapped Sara on the shoulder. "We seem to have an audience," he said with a chuckle.

Sara opened her eyes and looked out the window. Two small children, their faces smeared with chocolate, were standing on tiptoe peering in at them.

Sara sat straight up and tried to look dignified. At the same time, Brad put his hand on the steering wheel and started the engine. The two children jumped back from the car and ran off in the direction of their parents.

Brad turned to face Sara. "Where to, madam?" he asked gallantly.

Sara turned her head regally and replied with a mischievous grin, "I know this little out-of-the-way place. . . ."

Brad laughed as they raced toward the countryside.

We hope you enjoyed reading this book. All the titles currently available in the Sweet Dreams series are listed at the front of the book. They are all available at your local bookshop or newsagent, though should you find any difficulty in obtaining the books you would like, you can order direct from the publisher, at the address below. Also, if you would like to know more about the series, or would simply like to tell us what you think of the series, write to:

Kim Prior
Sweet Dreams
Transworld Publishers Ltd.
61–63 Uxbridge Road
Ealing
London W5 5SA

To order books, please list the title(s) you would like, and send together with a cheque or postal order made payable to TRANSWORLD PUBLISHERS LTD. Please allow the cost of the book(s) plus postage and packing charges as follows:

All orders up to a total of £5.00: 50p
All orders in excess of £5.00: Free

Please note that payment must be made in pounds sterling; other currencies are unacceptable.

(The above applies to readers in the UK and Republic of Ireland only)

If you live in Australia or New Zealand and would like more information about the series, please write to:

Sally Porter
Sweet Dreams
Transworld Publishers (Aust) Pty Ltd.
15-23 Helles Avenue
Moorebank
N.S.W. 2170
AUSTRALIA

Kiri Martin
Sweet Dreams
c/o Corgi and Bantam Books New Zealand
Cnr. Moselle and Waipareira Avenues
Henderson
Auckland
NEW ZEALAND